BOOK GIRL

and the Captive Fool

Mizuki Nomura

"Why are you eating the parts that I balled up and threw away?"

"They're simple and delicious."

Like getting the crusts of bread from a bakery, maybe? And e-e-every once in a while, there's a smudge of strawberry or blueberry jam still on it, and then I feel like I hit the jackpot."

Sarashina

Takeda

Kotobuki

"If a relationship is just going to fall apart some day, it's better not to get involved at all."

I couldn't hear any more of this.
Once I heard it, I could never
pretend that I hadn't.

Contents

BOOK girl

and the Captive Fool

Mizuki Nomura

Illustrations by Miho Takeoka

Yen
Press

NEW YORK

BOOK GIRL AND THE CAPTIVE FOOL
Story: MIZUKI NOMURA
Illustrations: MIHO TAKEOKA

Translation by Karen McGillicuddy

Bungakushoujo to tsunagareta fool © 2006 Mizuki Nomura. All rights reserved. First published in Japan in 2006 by ENTERBRAIN, INC., Tokyo. English translation rights arranged with ENTER-BRAIN, INC. through Tuttle-Mori Agency, Inc., Tokyo.

English translation © 2011 by Hachette Book Group, Inc.

Yen Press
Hachette Book Group
237 Park Avenue, New York, NY 10017

www.HachetteBookGroup.com
www.YenPress.com.

Yen Press is an imprint of Hachette Book Group, Inc. The Yen Press name and logo are trademarks of Hachette Book Group, Inc.

First Yen Press Edition: July 2011

Library of Congress Cataloging-in-Publication Data
Nomura, Mizuki.
    [Bungakushoujo to tsunagareta fool. English]
    Book Girl and the captive fool / Mizuki Nomura ; illustrations by Miho Takeoka ; [translation by Karen McGillicuddy]. —1st Yen Press ed.
        p. cm.
    Summary : When Tohko, a goblin who is also known as Book Girl because she loves literature so much that she actually devours it, discovers a library book with pages sliced out, she also learns of the darkness in the heart of one of her classmates.
    ISBN 978-0-316-07693-7
    [1. Mystery and detective stories.   2. Books and reading—Fiction.   3. Goblins—Fiction.   4. Japan—Fiction.]   I. Takeoka, Miho, ill.   II. McGillicuddy, Karen.   III. Title.
    PZ7.N728Bn 2011
    [Fic] —dc22   2010044317

10 9 8 7 6 5 4 3 2 1

RRD-C

Printed in the United States of America

and the Captive Fool

Mizuki Nomura
Illustrations by Miho Takeoka

This letter is my warning to you.
You have to get away, please.
Every time you rest your sweet, poison-laden hands on my heart, you send it reeling and my spirit thrums crazily. I can't control the destructive impulses that surge through me. I tremble with a desire to cut you apart. When I close my eyes, all I see — night or day — is you.
I yearn to cut your spiteful gaze apart — that pale, dignified face you turn on me, your slender, arrogant throat — to carve away your ears and nose, to dig your eyeballs out of your head. My heart cries out to etch a crucifix into your supple chest and to paint your entire body in fountains of warm blood.
You have to get away.
I know I'll cut you apart.

Prologue – Memories for an Introduction – I Used to Be a Fool in Love

She was too pure, too beautiful…

There was a fledgling scriptwriter who paid tribute to the woman he loved with those words, but when I was in middle school, I was trapped in a mire of passion that made his pale in comparison.

When I woke in the mornings, my first thought was of Miu's face. Her tea-colored almond eyes and her plump lips. The rustle of her brown hair tied up in a high ponytail.

Miu always peeked at me with teasing, playful looks.

Good morning, Konoha.

Good morning, Miu.

Every morning I would greet the Miu of my imagination. Her eyes would crinkle with her smile, and joy would shoot through my heart. I would head to the bathroom in a haze of nervous excitement, eager to get to school so I could see the real Miu just one minute — one second — sooner.

How would Miu smile at me today? Would she be teasing me today? How far had she gotten in the story she was writing? I wanted to see her! I wanted to hear her voice and see her smile.

I couldn't wait to get to school, and I would linger under a sycamore along the way until Miu came. When she appeared, bathed in pure light, her ponytail bobbing, I would pretend that I had only just gotten there and run up to her shouting, "Miu! Miu!"

She was all I could think about during classes, too. When her seat was behind mine, I would turn around constantly during the day, and the sight of her bangs falling across her forehead or of her lowered lashes never failed to send a thrill through my heart. When we changed seats and her desk was diagonally in front of me, I never grew tired of gazing at the slender taper of her neck or her profile that reminded me of a budding flower.

Miu usually had a sky blue binder open in front of her, writing a story on loose-leaf paper.

Writing out the dreamlike world she was creating...

The beautiful words that flashed and danced like light on the page.

When they streamed from Miu's lips, the words shone even fresher and more beautiful, driving me ever deeper into my dreams.

You're special, you know. I'm only showing this to you, Konoha.

Every word Miu spoke to me was sweet like sugar drops.

Back then, I was walking on air, an utter fool for love; with her smiles washing over me, I was an incorrigible dreamer.

I assumed that Miu would, of course, feel the same way about me, and I never doubted even for a moment that we were bound together by destiny.

Even after we started high school, even after we went to college, even after we got jobs, Miu would be at my side, writing her stories and calling my name with a teasing smile. And that wasn't all. Some day Miu would become a real author, and everyone would know how good she was. That's what I believed.

*   *   *

4

But in the spring of our last year of middle school, I debuted under the pen name of Miu Inoue as a brilliant, mysterious author who happened to be a lovely fourteen-year-old girl, and I lost Miu.

And now, in my second year of high school...
...I'm a perfectly normal high school boy, going to class like anyone else, and I go to the book club's room after school and write "snacks" for my not-at-all-normal club president.

Chapter 1 – Don't Leave a Crumb

"*Tomb of the Wild Chrysanthemum* tastes like freshly picked apricots," Tohko murmured affectionately as she flipped through a collection of stories she'd borrowed from the library. "It reminds me of being on a footpath bathed in the light of the setting sun, plucking a rouged apricot between your fingers, then popping it into your mouth and sloooowly biting into it. Its thin skin ruptures, and a gentle tang and joyous sweetness seep across your tongue as your heart squeezes tight at the forlorn bitterness of it! Ahhh, the sweetly ephemeral memories of a boy's first love!

"The author of *Tomb of the Wild Chrysanthemum* was Sachio Ito, who was a disciple of Shiki Masaoka. He published the story in the magazine *Little Cuckoo* in 1906. It was acclaimed by the great Sōseki Natsume. The classics really are wonderful! It's like how apricots produce different fruit every year — it's fresh and delicious every time, no matter how often you eat it!"

Sitting at the old oak table, I wrote Tohko's improv story in a notebook.

I guess Tohko was really into old Japanese love stories lately, because yesterday she had read Ogai's "The Dancing Girl" and before that Yasunari Kawabata's "The Izu Dancer" and before that Ichiyō Higuchi's *Growing Up,* and she'd expounded passionately on them all.

"That's school property. You can't eat it," I warned her placidly as my pencil raced over the page.

"I *know* that!" she answered, pouting. She had "accidentally" eaten a library book before, and she'd whined that she was too embarrassed to go apologize on her own, so she'd forced me, her lackey, to go with her.

She gave a desolate sigh immediately after. "But it looks soooo good. Argh!"

She was like a toddler looking in the window of an ice cream parlor and nibbling covetously on her fingers.

"No eating it."

"I know, I know! Augh, this part here? It's ever so slightly tart and totally delicious!"

"I'm serious. You can't have any."

"Fiiiine," she replied lazily, her face like that of a cat basking in the sun. "I'll just wait until your snack is ready, like a good girl."

The room stood at the far western end of the school building and was extremely cramped, stacked all over with mounds of old books. Tohko had set her fold-up chair next to the window, and she sat with her legs drawn up on it, awash in the autumn sunlight streaming in the window as she paged through her book with slender fingers. Her white kneecaps peeked out from under her pleated skirt, and her long, black braids that looked like cats' tails spilled over her shoulders.

Tohko is a goblin who eats stories.

She rips up books or pieces of paper with words written on them, pops them into her mouth, and munches away at them, then swallows primly.

She seemed to be deeply upset at being categorized as a "goblin," and she would plant her hands on her hips and declare, "I am not a goblin. I'm just a book girl."

And certainly, there was something about her that was reminiscent of an old-fashioned, unsullied maiden…if you ignored her extraordinary bibliophilism and the fact that she adored books so much that she ate them up with satisfied crinkling.

We were the only members of the Seijoh Academy book club: Tohko, in her third year, and I, in my second.

Autumn was half over, and other clubs were already starting to hand over responsibilities to their younger members. Was Tohko ever going to step aside? Seijoh was a ticket to college, so she *must* have been taking entrance exams…But she didn't seem to be studying at all. Was she going to be okay? She couldn't be planning on repeating a year in order to stick around, could she…?

I was beginning to grow uneasy when Tohko started talking to me.

"Next month is the culture fair. My class is running a curry restaurant. What's yours doing?"

"We're doing a manga café. All we have to do is line up the desks and chairs, get some instant coffee and tea bags, then put out manga, so it's no big deal. I don't really care about stuff like the culture fair or field day, so I'm fine with that."

"You shouldn't be so aloof. It makes you sound like an old man."

"I think a high schooler who thought the culture fair was the most important thing in the world would be more unusual, actually."

"If you keep looking so bored with everything, your face is going to freeze that way."

Tohko pouted and turned the pages of her book. Then suddenly, she shouted, "Hey!!"

It happened just as I set down the final period in her snack, so I looked up in surprise.

What was it? What had happened?

Tohko held the book in both hands, her eyes bulging, and she trembled uncontrollably.

"Th-there are pages missing from this book. The most famous line is missing — it never said 'You're like a chrysanthemum, Tami.' Their banter is completely gone. But that's the best part! It was so unaffected! Oh my god, you can see where they cut it ooouuutttt! Who would do that?!"

"...Tohko." I sighed and put a hand to my head.

"Wh-why are you acting so disgusted, Konoha? You don't think *I* ate it, do you?!"

"I warned you over and over not to eat school property...ugh, why me?"

"No! It wasn't me! I've been with you this whole time, so I'm innocent!"

"You didn't tear it out and sneak a bite while I was writing your snack, did you?"

"So you really do suspect your president! How could you?! I wouldn't do that! Even if a bookstore or library has superdelicious books on display and I happen to wander in when I'm hungry and even if my stomach starts grumbling just from the sight of the covers, I don't *do* anything!" she declared firmly, puffing up her flat chest.

"Besides, it's so crass to pick out all the best parts and just leave the rest. I eat everything, from the very beginning to the very end. That's just being polite to the author."

I couldn't argue with that. Tohko would happily devour any book straight through to the end. When I sometimes wrote improv stories that didn't suit her palate, she would whine that they were too spicy or too bitter, but she would choke down every last scrap.

"No, I wouldn't expect a glutton like you to leave anything

behind," I murmured in agreement, and her mouth pulled down into a sour frown and her eyes turned petulant.

"I don't hear any respect for your club president there."

Then she closed her book and leaped up from her chair, valiantly declaring, "Anyway! I refuse to overlook someone only eating the best part! I was saving it for last. It's like sneaking all the ginkgo nuts out of egg custard! It's like stealing all the strawberries off a shortcake! Like picking all the shrimp out of a seafood gratin! It's the act of a devil, stealing the moment of joy you've been waiting for out from under you and casting you instead into a pit of despair! The enemy of all gastronomes—I mean, of all readers! The enemy of the book club! We've got to stop this criminal and put the screws to them, no matter what. This is a top priority investigation, Konoha!"

I was afraid this would happen. I hated getting dragged into Tohko's detective games all the time. Unbelievable. I tore my steaming-fresh improv story out of the notebook and held it out to Tohko.

"I'm done writing your snack. You want to save it?"

Tohko had been on the verge of flying out of the room, but she pulled to a halt.

"Er…"

Today's prompts had been "Musashi Miyamoto," "heated carpet," and "dancing at the Obon festival in the summer." Before I'd started writing, Tohko had hugged the back of her chair and excitedly dictated, "Autumn requires chestnuts. Write me a story like a Mont Blanc made from Japanese chestnuts!"

But I had no idea what it would taste like.

I dangled the pages from my fingertips, and Tohko gazed at them covetously, like a horse confronted with a carrot.

Finally, she plunked back into her seat and held out both hands with a beatific smile.

"I'll have it now. Thank you!"

Addendum:

Tohko polished off the Mont Blanc–like improv I wrote, shrieking, "Oh noooo! Musashi Miyamoto is having a show-down with a heated carpet and the Obon dancing!! The heated carpet rolled up around him and burnt him to a crisp! The chest-nut paste is too hot and goopy. There's radish where the chestnuts should be! And there's mayonnaise on top. It's soooo grooooss. Urk — ugh … bleh …"

In the end, she covered her mouth with a hand and fell back limply against her fold-up chair, so the investigation was put on hold and I sidestepped the danger.

The next day was a beautiful, clear autumn day.

Tohko had seemed pretty beat up the day before, so I wondered if she'd made it home all right. With that thought running through my mind, I stepped into my classroom and ran straight into my classmate Kotobuki.

"Oh —"

"I-Inoue!"

Kotobuki had been on her way out to the hall, but she suddenly recoiled and her face tensed.

I put on a fresh smile ready for public consumption and tried to give her a friendly greeting.

"Morning, Kotobuki."

She glared at me then, her eyes reproachful. "Same anemic smile as always. How can you be so flippant with every single person you talk to, Inoue? Get out of my way."

Then she walked off quickly.

I'd heard that Kotobuki had covered for me while she was in the hospital during the summer and that had made me think that maybe she wasn't so bad, but the second term had started now, and she was still acting the same as ever. She'd always been a harsh beauty and had never been a very friendly person, but I felt like her natural personality was even worse around me and that she gave me her prickliest looks and comments.

Had it just been a hallucination when I saw Kotobuki hang her head and look like she was about to cry in her hospital bed? What she'd said that day had been nagging at me, but I could hardly ask her about it.

Sighing, I set my bag on my desk, and my classmate Akutagawa came over.

"Morning, Inoue."

"Oh, morning, Akutagawa."

I guess Akutagawa had seen that exchange with Kotobuki. "Don't let her bother you," he reassured me.

"Thanks, but you're a little late for that."

"Oh."

"Yeah. If Kotobuki suddenly started being nice, I think I'd keel over in shock. Oh, hey, can I check my math homework with yours?"

We opened our notebooks on my desk and exchanged brief conversation. Akutagawa's notebooks were always perfectly organized and easy to read. His sober, tranquil personality came through even in his handwriting.

He was tall with broad shoulders and cool, masculine features, and he was calm, honorable, and balanced — Akutagawa was a lot of things I wished I could be. We weren't close enough that I would call him a friend, but it felt comfortable being around him.

Just then, Akutagawa's pants pocket vibrated.

"'Scuse me."

He pulled out his cell phone, checked the screen, and frowned.

His face was dark as he glowered at the display, and there was something threatening in the air around him that made my heart skip a beat.

13

Akutagawa muttered another apology in a steely voice and went out into the hall.

Who could that call have been from?

His family? A friend? Maybe a girlfriend?

But he'd never mentioned anything about a girl before. He was such a placid person that his look of momentary loathing unnerved me. So even Akutagawa could look like that...

I never imagined that that would be the start of all the trouble.

I was walking down the hall during lunch when I felt someone looking at me.

"Um, Inoue?"

A weak voice had called out my name, and I turned around to see a meek-looking girl with glossy hair pouring down her back.

Wait — I think this girl is in my grade. I didn't know her name, but I'd seen her occasionally. She was pretty, so she left an impression. I wondered what she wanted from me.

The girl looked like she was bursting with nervous energy.

"I'm sorry to stop you like this. Um, my name is Sarashina. I'm in class three. You're... Kazushi's friend, right?"

"Who's Kazushi?"

"Oh, I'm sorry." Her pale cheeks flushed red. "I mean the boy in your class, Kazushi Akutagawa. I'm going out with him."

She was Akutagawa's girlfriend?

I was so shocked, I stared back at her skeptically. Sarashina watched me with a look of desperation on her face. Her hair was lushly soft, and her face seemed pure and kind — a perfect honor student beauty. She would be a perfect match for Akutagawa.

This was the first I'd heard of Akutagawa having a girlfriend. I knew lots of girls liked him, and just recently there had been a cute, light blue envelope stuck into one of his textbooks. I'd asked him if it was a love letter, but he mumbled something and seemed uncomfortable.

Since Akutagawa and I were the kind of acquaintances who didn't even know much about each other's families, it wasn't that strange to find out that he had a girlfriend.

"Er...I'm sorry. I didn't know he had a girlfriend."

Suddenly Sarashina's face clouded over. *Oops—maybe I shouldn't have said that.*

"...So Kazushi hasn't mentioned me to you."

"Well, I mean, Akutagawa and I aren't really that close..."

I tried to correct myself quickly, but Sarashina didn't seem to hear me.

"Kazushi has been acting strangely lately. It seems like he's avoiding me...I wonder if there's another girl that he likes."

I saw tears gathering in her black eyes and didn't know what to do. I was terrible at stuff like this. I tried to say something nice, though.

"Are you sure it's not a misunderstanding? I don't think Akutagawa's the type to cheat on a girl. If it's bothering you, maybe you should ask him about it?"

Sarashina's eyes teared up even more when I said that, and she fixed her gaze on at me.

"Could you ask him for me, Inoue?"

"What?"

"I'm too scared to ask him myself. And you're his friend, so he'll probably tell you the truth. Please, Inoue? You'd be doing me a huge favor."

I caved. How did I always get dragged into things?

After classes ended, I was struggling with how to broach the subject with Akutagawa.

15

"Bye, Inoue."

Akutagawa was leaving the room. Oh no! I rushed after him.

What else could I do? Better to get bad stuff over with quickly. I would just ask casually, so things didn't get all serious.

Akutagawa, are you dating anyone right now? A girl I know wanted me to ask you, so...

But as he strode ahead, I couldn't close the distance between us at all. Akutagawa belonged to the archery team and had been first-string at the practices since his first year. I thought he was going to the practice hall, but then he turned into the library.

He went past the front desk until coming to a stop in the dimly lit corner at the very back, where they kept the Japanese literature, and began rummaging through the books. He would take a book off the shelf, riffle through the pages, then put it back.

He seemed intent on choosing the right book, but maybe he was looking for something?

Maybe it was my stress that made the area seem oddly quiet to the point that I was sure Akutagawa would hear me gulping. I hesitated to call out to him, squelching my breath and standing behind a shelf. Just then, Akutagawa took a fold-up box cutter out of the book bag slung over his shoulder.

Wait, what?

He pulled the blade open with his fingertips. My eyes caught the gleaming edge.

What was he doing?

I realized he was acting strangely, and my palms started to sweat. I held my breath and didn't even dare blink as I watched him. His expression grim, Akutagawa rested the tip of the blade on the book's center fold.

He wasn't—

My heart skipped a beat.

He drew the blade down the page with a practiced motion, and I flinched, as if the blade had pierced my own skin.

The image of Tohko pouting and holding *Tomb of the Wild Chrysanthemum* out in front of me yesterday came vividly to mind.

The pages that weren't where they were supposed to be and the mark of a knife...

Was Akutagawa the one who'd damaged the book?!

I grabbed hold of a shelf. My fingers brushed a book and knocked it into the book beside it, making a slight sound.

Akutagawa turned around, his eyes wide, and he stared at me blankly.

I stared back at him in disbelief.

Akutagawa's brow furrowed in pain.

My head was numb with heat, my thoughts utterly mired.

"Akutagawa, why are you..."

I managed to get the words out somehow.

Just then, the sleeve of a girl's school uniform reached past me and a fist boldly caught the hand in which Akutagawa held the knife.

"I got you! Caught in the act!"

The school uniform belonged to the book girl, her long braids swaying like cats' tails as she leaped out, her breathing wild — it was Tohko, president of the book club.

———⟩◆⟨———

Ever since that day when I was made aware of the fact that I'm a contemptible, inferior person, I've worked hard to be honorable toward the people around me.

Ever since that evil day when everything was torn apart, drenched in blood, and passed away to a place I couldn't reach,

I've tried to act diligently to avoid making foolish choices again.

I hoped I would be able to face your wish with sincerity.

Whenever I think of what you must have felt, what it must have cost you to write this letter, my heart feels like it's on fire and I feel compelled to do whatever I can.

But your demands are too cruel. I pushed my sincerity to its limits as best I could and gave the best response I was capable of, but even so, I doubt you were satisfied.

I can't give you what you wish for. That would be the insincere act of a demon and would lead to the ruin of everything.

———⟹◆⟸———

"Now then, why were you cutting up library books? Start explaining yourself."

Back in the book club room, which was overtaken by old books, Tohko was trying to act threatening, like the bad cop in a TV show. A book of stories by Takeo Arishima lay on the rough surface of our wobbly oak table with the pages that had been cut out arrayed next to it.

Akutagawa was sitting in a chair, hanging his head in silence.

Yesterday, Tohko had gotten sick after eating my snack and had declared the investigation open. She had been keeping watch at the library in order to catch the slasher right after classes.

"It looks like my gut was right. The guilty always return to the scene of the crime. Skipping out on cleaning duty and battling hunger while I hid behind that shelf for thirty minutes paid off."

She sounded so self-important, I felt myself getting a headache.

Tohko had dragged Akutagawa straight back to the club room.

"The part you cut out was a scene from 'A Bunch of Grapes.'"

The boy has stolen the art supplies of a classmate, and his deed is revealed in front of everyone. The teacher takes him aside, and just as he feels ready to burst with shame, the teacher places a bunch of grapes on his lap and comforts him — it's a famous, heartwarming scene! It's the most delicious scene in this story! Have you ever imagined the pain and the sorrow of the person who's forced to just eat the skins of grapes without anything inside them?"

Tohko's voice was shaking, as if this situation was utterly unprecedented.

"I don't think your average high schooler *has* thought about that, actually," I interjected, and she glared at me.

"You stay out of it, Konoha.

"I don't care if he is your friend. As a book girl, if food is dese-crated at his hands — I mean, if he damages the sanctity of the written word, I can hardly overlook such an act. Why would you do something like that?"

"Well —"

As Akutagawa opened his mouth to answer, Tohko's voice sud-denly grew louder.

"This is my theory. To come right to the point, you are a devo-tee of naturalism. Your favorite book is *The Quilt* by Katai Tayama."

At this preposterous declaration, Akutagawa and I both turned and gaped at Tohko, whose nose was thrust confidently into the air.

"'A Bunch of Grapes,' which you rendered incorporeal, was written by Takeo Arishima, one of the literary men who congre-gated in the artists' group called the White Birch Society, and was published at the turn of the century. The counterpart to the White Birch Society, which loudly extolled humanitarianism and idealism, was the naturalists — literature which sought to describe reality objectively and which was personified by Katai Tayama. The White Birch Society actually arose from a rejection of naturalism. So it came to me: This is the reckless act of youth and love by a person who supports naturalism from the very bottom of his heart."

Tohko's imagination was what was reckless.

I slumped, but Akutagawa spoke up calmly beside me.

"You're mistaken, actually."

"What? I...I am?" Tohko blinked in wonder.

"Yes..."

An awkward silence filled the cramped room.

"So then, why did you cut up those books?"

She tilted her head in timid curiosity, and her long, thin braids spilled over her frail shoulders.

Apparently Tohko's confusion set him at ease, because Akutagawa sat up straighter and began to tell his story with an honorable set to his face.

"My midterm grades weren't what I was hoping for, and I was annoyed. I've had this desire to hurt something—to cut something up for a while...I thought that maybe cutting up a book would satisfy that urge, and so I tried it."

His grades weren't what he was hoping for? Hadn't he been fifth-highest ranked in our grade? And if you were participating in club activities at this school, wasn't that good enough? But maybe for Akutagawa, fifth was a failure that made him cringe in pain?

Tohko, who regularly bragged (?) that she had never gotten more than a thirty in math, also looked like she was having trouble believing him.

"You cut up a book because you got a bad grade?"

"Yes."

"That's it?"

20

"Yes."

"It really has nothing to do with naturalism?"

"Absolutely nothing."

Tohko's face drooped in disappointment, and she fiddled with the ends of her braids.

Akutagawa stood up, back still straight, and bowed his head deeply to us both.

"I'm sorry for causing you all this trouble. I'll go to the library to apologize and pay for the books I cut up."

He moved to leave the room, but Tohko called out to him, "Wait! If you regret what you did, there's no need to tell anyone it was you."

She smiled easily at Akutagawa as he turned back around, trying to break the tension.

"You'll still make it up, of course. Luckily, I have some pull with the library staff. I'll say some bugs chewed them up and the book club's alums donated new books, and they'll switch them out. It'll make the book club look good, too, so we both win."

I quickly nodded my agreement.

"Yeah, that's good. Let's do that, Akutagawa," I said.

Tohko could come in handy sometimes after all. I was just thinking about writing her a super-sweet story later when she continued.

"But! That isn't going to solve the problems you're facing. You need something more in order to free you from all your troubles, so you can savor your time in school with sunshiny feelings. And what you need is to throw yourself body and soul into a project with your friends. The vigor of youth will banish your stress to another world!"

There were some ominous signs developing. Akutagawa also frowned suspiciously.

Tohko flashed a grin at him.

"So, Akutagawa, why don't you participate in our play for the culture fair?"

After Akutagawa asked for time to think about this, looking utterly dumbfounded, and left the room, I rounded on Tohko.

"What are you talking about?! You never said anything about putting on a play for the culture fair!"

Tohko hugged the back of the fold-up chair and looked up at me joyously.

"But I already filed a request with the event board and got hold of a stage."

"You what?!"

"Well, Maki made a crack about how the orchestra is putting on a concert in their personal music hall, but the book club isn't doing anything again this year. And it hurt my feelings. Last year we didn't put out a single newsletter, and all we did was an exhibit of classical literature... And then nobody came, and all you did was goof off and do crossword puzzles."

Somewhere in there she started glaring and pouting at me. I was fed up.

"The reason we didn't have a single newsletter was because you ate them all."

"Are you sure? Well, anyway, I can't lose to the orchestra this year just because they have more people. Besides, someone might see our play at the fair and find out how amazing we are and join the club."

Given those choices, the latter was probably the more urgent problem. Tohko had been worried for a while about how few people were in the club and had told me, "You're a good-for-nothing, Konoha, so the club could fall apart once I graduate. How could I live with myself?

"Listen, Konoha. This is an order from your president. As a

member of the book club, you're going to make the club look good at the fair and bring your A-game to ensure we get at least one new member."

And there it was! Tohko's "presidential order." I didn't want to draw attention to myself—all I wanted was to live my life in peace.

"Can we really put on a play when there's just the two of us?"

A smile flashed over Tohko's face.

"That's why I asked Akutagawa, of course. Ever since I decided that we would perform in the culture fair, I've had my eye on him. I figured he would draw in the female crowd. I was going to get you to talk him into it, but he saved us a lot of trouble. One more benefit of my innate virtues, I guess."

That had no connection whatsoever to Akutagawa's problems. It was just Tohko looking out for her own best interests. But Tohko had seized on his weakness and was trying to drag him into this inexplicable play. I felt sorry for Akutagawa.

"Exactly what kind of play are we doing?" I asked warily.

"As befits the book club, it's going to be a major literary work, of course. Melancholy and delicious and rich with the vigor of youth! I thought it would be neat if the costumes were from just before the turn of the century, so this last week I've been scouring the choices."

And then all she'd read was romances?

Tohko got up from her chair and took a book from the pile and loudly proclaimed, "And so I chose this—*Love and Death* by Saneatsu Mushanokōji!"

"Mushanokōji?" I asked, remembering something I'd learned in class. "Isn't he from the White Birch Society, too?"

Tohko nodded enthusiastically. "That's right! It feels almost fated that Akutagawa cut up a book by Takeo Arishima, who's also in the White Birch Society!"

I wish she wouldn't call that fate…

Tohko seized that opportunity to go into greater detail.

"Saneatsu Mushanokōji was born on May 12, 1885 — the eighteenth year of the Meiji era — the youngest child of minor nobility. But despite that, his father died young, and as the family wasn't exactly wealthy, they were forced to live frugally.

"He progressed to an academy, where he met Naoya Shiga, and the two of them published a magazine together called *The White Birch*. As the key figures in the magazine, they left behind a great many works that forcefully evoke the beauty and goodness humanity possesses. If you think youth, you have to think White Birch Society! Democracy at the dawn of the century!

"Naoya Shiga is called the god of fiction, and he left us famous works like 'At Cape Kinosaki' and 'The Errand Boy's God,' written in an intellectual style, which was pared down to its barest elements! Takeo Arishima, who described human destiny and emotion with searing phrases that gushed like blood! Ton Satomi, who used rich psychological description and a rhythmic style to establish a 'philosophy of sincerity,' which devoted the body to the desires of one's own heart!

"If the writing of Naoya Shiga is the ultimate soba made by a famous chef to be both chewy and smooth going down the throat, then Takeo Arishima's work would be a gooey raw oyster with lemon spritzed over it. Ton Satomi tastes kind of like boiled potatoes that are perfectly smooth on the outside. They're all tasty enough to make my tongue tremble, and I always eat too much. Arishima's *The Agony of Coming into the World* and Satomi's *A Carefree Fellow* are must-reads.

"And *this* is the person who absolutely must not be overlooked! Saneatsu Mushanokōji! For me, Mushanokōji *is* the White Birch Society. People tend to think that because of his grandiose name and the fact that he's from a noble family, the things he writes must also be impenetrable and difficult. But when they actually come into contact with his work, they're shocked at how entertaining and easy to read they are.

"The special appeal of Mushanokōji has got to be how much dialogue he uses and how buoyant it is. He often has long lines that take up an entire page, but there's rhythm in everything and you can read it all effortlessly! If I had to compare it to something, I would say Mushanokōji's works are like tofu from a high-end Japanese restaurant. The texture is refreshing and light while the soy flavor brings out an exquisite sweetness and depth, and then you get the lingering taste of the coagulant, and the moment you've polished off the very last bite, you sigh and think, *My gosh that was delicious.*"

She closed her eyes, and I thought she really was going to sigh, but then she snapped her eyes open and drew her face closer enthusiastically.

"Out of everything he wrote, the heroine of *Love and Death*, Natsuko, is one of the loveliest heroines in the history of Japanese literature.

"She's pure and refreshing like alabaster tofu, delicious even if you eat it plain with no toppings at all! She exchanges letters with the main character, who's gone to study abroad, and her writing is *so* artless, it sends a jolt through your heart. Oh, and — and — the scene where she appears is so cute and adorable!! A bunch of girls are gathered in a garden having a handstand competition. Natsuko is famous for her handstands, and she even does a flip. At the celebration for her older brother's birthday, she executes an amazing flip, and the guests shower her with applause!"

"Hold on a second!"

I forced my way into Tohko's unflagging discourse.

"A heroine who does a flip? That's never going to happen! Who's going to do that?"

25

"But anyone can stand on her head at least! And Natsuko says that she practiced doing somersaults and then just naturally started doing flips. It'll be fine."

Tohko smiled carelessly, but I cut in sharply. "No way. Or at least, no way for someone who gets hit in the face by volleyballs, or gets tangled in the net when she tries to spike, or who hits herself in the head with the bat when she swings in softball, or who tries to show off doing the butterfly in swim class, but her legs cramp up and she drowns in the pool like you do. Totally impossible."

Tohko flushed bright red.

"How exactly are you witnessing all of these embarrassing things happening to me?"

"Because you're always doing embarrassing stuff. I just want you to accept that you have zero athletic ability. You'll never be able to do a handstand or a flip."

That seemed to infuriate Tohko, and she pouted.

"That's not true. As long as I have my love for the book club, I'll be able to do it."

"Does the book club have anything to do with it?"

"Sure. My love for the story makes anything possible. One or two handstands is nothing. I'll show you the power of my love."

I saw she was going to try to do a handstand against the wall, and I panicked.

"Don't do that! What if you hurt yourself? Besides, if you flip over in those clothes, your skirt is going to fall down and you're going to flash your underwear."

"I'm wearing gym shorts, don't worry. Open your eyes and get a load of *this!*"

Tohko raised both hands high overhead and kicked off powerfully toward the wall.

"Waugh! Tohko, stop!"

Her full pleated skirt flipped over and her pale, thin legs stretched into the air.

As soon as I caught a glimpse of the black shorts covering her tiny butt, her extended legs reeled forward and she screamed.

"Eeeek!"

"L-look out!"

I grabbed at Tohko's ankles but only managed to catch her right leg, and we both toppled into a pile of books.

The stack of books fell down around us like an avalanche, dust and mold billowing up on all sides. Then the collapsed mound of books knocked over the pile that had been next to it, and the pile next to *that* one collapsed, too, until it was a total massacre, scattering all the books in the tiny room.

Tohko was flat on her back, buried under a ton of books, sneezing every time she breathed in the dust. Tears were in her eyes as she said, "Ahchoo! I guess we should do a different story after all."

Wasn't there any way I could get Tohko to give up on performing a play?

The next day, I sat at my desk in class with an anxious look on my face, thinking this over, when Akutagawa came over to stand in front of me.

I sat up straighter reflexively. With his typical quiet expression, Akutagawa said, "Sorry for putting you and Amano through all that yesterday."

I was relieved to hear his placid tone and gave him the same smile I always did.

"Don't worry about it. I was surprised, but I suppose everyone gets annoyed at something."

Yes! If I told Tohko that Akutagawa wouldn't be in the play, she might give up on the idea, too.

I leaned forward.

27

"About the play — Tohko is just letting the idea run away with her. You don't have to do it. Do you want me to talk to her?"

But Akutagawa looked earnest as he said, "No, I've decided to do it. I'm a boring person without any training as an actor, so I might just get in your way. But I intend to give it my best effort. I hope that's all right."

...He... *WHAT?!*

When I saw the troupe gathered in the tiny club room after school, my eyes bugged out yet again.

"K-Kotobuki?! And... and Takeda?!"

"What's your problem? The only reason I'm doing this is because Tohko asked me to help. It's got nothing to do with you! Like I would ever want to do a scene with you."

Standing next to Kotobuki and her bitter assault was a petite girl with billowing hair, smiling cheerfully.

"Heh-heh. It sounded neat, so I'm on board!"

Takeda was a first-year student who worked in the library. I had ghostwritten love letters for her before and all sorts of stuff had happened, so now she dropped by the book club to visit from time to time.

Takeda looked up at me with friendly, puppylike eyes and inclined her head winsomely.

"Hold on! Konoha, your face is all tense. Don't you want to perform with me?"

"No, that's not —"

Kotobuki glared at me as I scrambled for an answer. Her look was much harsher than usual. It occurred to me that Kotobuki also worked in the library, so she and Takeda probably knew each other. And Kotobuki had once trashed Takeda as "a girl who could be the victim of some guy's Lolita fantasy."

Could we really do this? With this group?

A cold sweat was covering me when Akutagawa came to stand next to me with a serious look on his face. When she saw him, Takeda shrieked.

"Ohhh! Are you going to perform, too, Akutagawa? That's *SO. COOL*. My friends are going to be so totally jealous! You have a lot of fans in first year, too! Oh — my name's Chia Takeda. I used to watch the archery team a lot."

Akutagawa nodded benevolently. "Yeah, I remember. You even came with Inoue once or twice."

"That's right. We're friends."

She twined her arm around mine and giggled. Kotobuki had kept her face turned away, but she spun around with terrifying force to look at us.

"I hope you don't mind, either, Konoha. Oh — and try to get along with everyone, Nanase. Can I call you Nanase?"

"*NO,*" Kotobuki answered immediately, her eyebrows twitching.

Takeda was all smiles in response.

"Got it! Nanase it is, then!"

"I told you *no,* didn't I?"

"Eeee! Nanase, you're so scary!"

Takeda clung to me even tighter. When Kotobuki saw that, she looked like she was about to snap.

"Grrr…How long are you gonna keep your arm around her, Inoue?!"

"Uh, s-sorry!" I stammered.

Kotobuki unleashed her attack on me, and I quickly freed my arm from Takeda's. Takeda whined sadly.

"We're not elementary school kids in some pageant, so stop clinging to each other."

Kotobuki's face was scarlet, and she turned away sharply.

Akutagawa watched the whole exchange with a mature attitude.

And then there was Tohko, the cause of all this…

"So! Everyone gets along already! My vision was impeccable when I picked out this group."

She nodded, completely self-satisfied. I wanted to go home.

After we somehow crammed five chairs around the table and each of us sat down, we finally started discussing the play. Tohko proudly offered up an old hardcover book.

"And so, after much deliberation within the club, we have decided that the play will be Saneatsu Mushanokōji's *Friendship!*"

"Oh wow! That sounds sooo prestigious!" Takeda clapped wildly.

"After much deliberation"? All Tohko did was settle for the safe choice of Mushanokōji's most famous work after she couldn't pull off a handstand.

Tohko went on, unconcerned.

"*Friendship* was written as a serialized novel for the *Osaka Daily* newspaper in 1919. Have any of you read it?"

"No." "I sure haven't!" "Me, either."

Akutagawa, Takeda, and Kotobuki replied simultaneously.

"Then I'll give you a brief rundown of the story. The characters are the playwright Nojima; his friend Omiya, an author; Sugiko, the student that Nojima loves; Takeko, Sugiko's friend and Omiya's cousin; then there's Nakata, who's Sugiko's older brother and Nojima's friend; and Hayakawa, Nojima's rival for Sugiko's love. I suppose that's everyone.

"The story starts with the main character, Nojima, falling for Sugiko the first time he meets her. Nojima becomes convinced that Sugiko will be his wife, and he goes to his friend Nakata's house in order to see her and becomes blinded with love for her.

"Nojima only reveals these feelings to his best friend Omiya. Omiya is a virile, honorable man, and he listens to Nojima earnestly and offers him his support.

"But Sugiko prefers Omiya.

"Trapped between love and friendship, Omiya leaves to study abroad in order to fulfill the duty of friendship, but Sugiko writes him letter after letter. And so, finally unable to restrain his feelings for her, Omiya asks her to come away with him."

Takeda's eyes were wide.

"Woooow. So Nojima loses his girlfriend, and then his best friend deserts him, too? That's awful!"

"Yes. The last scene is poignant but extremely moving and powerful. Besides, it's so stirring the way Nojima swings between joy and despair in his love for Sugiko. Look, look—isn't this scene wonderful? Nojima writes Sugiko's name in the sand, and he prays that if the letters don't disappear until the waves wash over it ten times, she'll return his feelings. It's *so* romantic!"

Tohko flipped open to a page as she described the scene.

Takeda and Kotobuki leaned in on either side of her to look.

The three of them pressed together so closely their heads were almost touching, and they leafed through the book, skimming it and saying things like, "Oh! This part is the best!" or "But what about *this* scene?"

At first Tohko was unchallenged as she argued heatedly for Nojima. "See? See? Isn't Nojima adorable? You can totally understand how he feels, like the world completely changes when you like somebody." But soon Kotobuki and Takeda started to argue with her.

"Whaaaat? But Tohko, Nojima gets way too carried away."

"I agree! If a boy loved me that passionately, I might back off. Nojima acts like a total girlie schoolgirl."

"You, you think? Isn't this normal if you're in love?"

"But in her letters to Omiya, even Sugiko is like, 'I'd rather die than marry Nojima,' or 'I don't want to be alone with Nojima for more than an hour.'"

"I totally get that. Nojima is obnoxious. He just starts treating

32

Sugiko like she's his wife, and if she even talks to another man, he gets all angry and says, 'That woman should be fed to the pigs. She is unworthy of my love.' Who does this guy think he is?"

"Seriously! He wants to be the only one Sugiko needs, and he's in this fantasy where he's an emperor and she's the queen. Of course, Sugiko would try to get away from that!"

"For sure."

The two of them had suddenly found themselves on the same wavelength, but Tohko continued to desperately defend Nojima.

"What?! But that's what's so cute about him! When people fall in love, they construct all these stories in their minds and get fluttery and excited. But at the same time, they have no self-confidence and get irritable and depressed, and they take their stress out on people like a little kid would.

"If the person they like so much likes them back, they can become much better people than they are. They could even rule the world. That happiness you feel, like your heart is soaring up to heaven, and then that anxiety when you want to cry because you come back to your senses. Nojima is genuinely running in panicked circles between those emotions. *I* think he's very straightforward and cute and wonderful anyway."

Tohko smiled.

"That may be your opinion, Tohko," Kotobuki replied crisply, "but I just can't get behind it. If you indulge boys who get these delusions, they're just going to get more intense."

"Hundred percent! I agree! Compared to him, Omiya is smooth and a*may*zing. Like when he defeats Sugiko at Ping-Pong — he's just too hot for words!"

"Yeah." Kotobuki nodded, looking triumphant. "Omiya's a great guy. The things he says when he's about to go abroad make me want to cry."

"Come onnnn! You have to appreciate Nojima's charms! You guys!"

I was impressed that they could get this worked up over a fictional character. Unable to jump into the girls' discussion, Akutagawa and I were staring at them blankly when Takeda brought it back around to us.

"Konoha, Akutagawa — what do you two think?"

"What—? Uh...Nojima definitely didn't pick up on Sugiko's hints. But I'm not sure how I feel about Omiya putting his letters to Sugiko in that magazine and then telling Nojima out of nowhere to go read them."

Then Akutagawa spoke up in a firm voice.

"I think Omiya shouldn't have accepted Sugiko. It doesn't matter what his reasons were. A person with any honor wouldn't betray his friend's trust."

Akutagawa's face was as harshly clenched as his voice. His eyes flashed, too, fixed on a point in space.

Takeda and Kotobuki both gaped at the sudden humorlessness.

I was flustered, too. *What happened, Akutagawa?!*

Just as things were starting to get uncomfortable, Tohko rested her hands on the table and leaned toward us.

"Oh, really! It's only because upstanding men of honor have been tormented that thrilling literature was born. If Omiya were a womanizing playboy, he never would have sweated his correspondence with Sugiko. This scene is one of my favorites. Bring me one more block of tofu! No, make it three! Four! No, bring me everything you've got! With a heap of ginger on top! Like that?"

I pressed a hand to my forehead.

"That comparison is too obscure, Tohko."

Akutagawa was flabbergasted, and Kotobuki and Takeda looked confused.

Tohko extended her right index finger, and wagging it back

34

and forth, she cheerfully declared, "Heh-heh, well! To put it simply, it's like you're com*plete*ly full, but you keep on eating anyway."

"I don't get it. But whatever, let's move on. We're running out of time."

She craned back to look at the clock on the wall, and her eyes widened. "Oh no, you're right! Let's pick roles, then. Konoha should probably be Nojima, and maybe Akutagawa should be Omiya?"

"No, I can't play the lead," I answered immediately. I was under enough pressure just appearing in a play; there was no way I could do *that*.

"Hmm. I think that's the obvious way to go, too."

"Yeah. You and Akutagawa are the only boys we have, so don't grumble and just do it."

"You want me to be Nojima?" Akutagawa offered.

"You can't do that! Omiya has that tall, handsome image. If Nojima is the cool one, it's not convincing for Sugiko to fall for Omiya instead," Takeda said sensibly. But wait — she was insulting me, wasn't she?

Then Tohko spoke up in a bright voice.

"All right! As the president of the book club, I will take on the role of Nojima!"

"What? You?!"

"Oh wow, a beautiful woman dressed like a boy? Like a Takarazuka?"

Kotobuki's and Takeda's eyes were wide.

Akutagawa looked surprised, too, and my mind was reeling. Sure, with her impoverished chest, Tohko could dress like a man even without using binding, but...

"Trust me. The book girl will give a masterful rendition of Nojima. So you'll be Omiya, right, Akutagawa?"

"Yes, if you want."

He nodded.

"Great! Thanks! I wanted you to be in the play no matter what, so when you came, I thought I'd hit the jackpot."

I couldn't believe she'd said that to him. She had a dreamy smile on her face. Tohko was pretty assertive about it, but had she really wanted to secure the female audience at the culture fair that badly? Akutagawa gave her an uncomfortable, awkward, ambiguous smile.

"Okay, next is the heroine Sugiko."

"Oh, oh! I nominate Nanase!!"

"Hey! Don't say that, Takeda!"

Kotobuki was thrown off guard.

"I think you'd be perfect! I mean, Sugiko has to be someone that Nojima would fall in love with instantly!"

"B-but...I mean, I can't act and..."

"Chia is right, Nanase. You would make an excellent Sugiko. You will do it, won't you? Please?"

Tohko rested a hand on Kotobuki's shoulder, and she choked, her face bright red. After stealing two or three quick glances at me, she answered in an embarrassed whisper, "O-okay..."

"You can do it, Kotobuki," I said.

I was trying to be encouraging, but her reticence sharpened instantaneously. She turned away and emphatically declared, "The fact that I accepted the role has nothing to do with *you*, Inoue."

"O-okay."

After that, it was decided that Takeda would be Takeko, Sugiko's friend and Omiya's cousin, and that I would be Hayakawa, Nojima's rival for Sugiko's love. At first I was relieved, thinking I wouldn't have a whole lot to do that way, but then Tohko sternly informed me that I would be writing the script.

36

"We need it by next Monday. I expect good things from you, Konoha."

Monday is only five days away! She's so rough on her underclassmen.

School was over.

I checked *Friendship* out of the library and went outside, where the walls of the school and the cherry trees on the campus were dyed by the brilliance of the setting sun. I felt the cold air of autumn on my cheek as I passed through the school gate, the gold and scarlet light flowing in like waves.

I saw Akutagawa a little ways ahead of me.

He'd stopped his bike next to a red mailbox and was standing ramrod straight on the verge of mailing a letter. His face was dyed in the rich evening light with a touch of tension and angst in it that brought me to a stop.

Akutagawa looked down at a long white envelope with melancholy eyes, frowning slightly.

He stood that way for a few moments, then dropped his letter into the mailbox and got on his bike.

"Akutagawa?" I called out and ran up to him. He turned to look at me with a hint of embarrassment on his face. "You're heading home now, right?"

"Yeah. I just stopped by the team."

Akutagawa got off his bike, and the two of us walked together down the sunset street.

There was something on my mind, and I decided to ask him about it.

"Are you really sure about appearing in the play? You shouldn't let Tohko bother you, you know."

His handsome face still turned away, Akutagawa murmured in a soft voice that crept into my heart.

"Sorry for worrying you. But when Tohko asked me to do the play, it made me want to try something different than I normally do. I was stressed out about all this stuff and felt really scattered, so actually I'm glad she asked."

"Is this about your grades?"

His breath caught slightly.

I wasn't sure if I should be asking about this. Trying not to overstep any boundaries, trying not to disrupt the delicate balance we had, I chose my words carefully, knowing I was taking a risk and unsure of myself, as if I was stepping onto thin ice.

"Are you sure there isn't something else bothering you? Like girl problems? Or something?"

As soon as I said that, my heart rate increased, and I regretted it. If he acted upset at all...But his expression didn't change.

"Why would you think that?"

"Because girls are all over you. Do you have a girlfriend?"

I remembered Sarashina's face. Her long silky hair, her spotless, gentle countenance, her frail voice.

Please, I want you to ask Kazushi if there's another girl.

I didn't think that Akutagawa was the type of guy who would cheat, but...

"No."

His voice was a little hard when he answered.

"Oh. That's a surprise."

"It shouldn't be."

Maybe he didn't want me to know about Sarashina. Was he embarrassed? Or was there some other reason he couldn't talk about it?

"What about you, Inoue?"

"Me? No. Unlike you, I've never even had a girl ask me out."

"You and Amano seem pretty close. You're not together?"

I lurched.

"Cut it out. That, at least, is never going to happen. I'm Tohko's snack master—I mean, her gofer. She's always ordering me around. She abuses her underclassmen. She's a tyrant."

I made that much clear.

"I see. Then what about—" He started to say something, then muttered, "Never mind."

I wondered what he'd held back. What did he start to ask me?

"So what's your type, Akutagawa?"

I tried a more roundabout approach this time. Akutagawa bowed his head thoughtfully.

"I don't think I have a type, per se. But —"

He paused, and his eyes grew melancholy again.

"If a girl shows me a side of herself that surprises me, I'm hooked. Like if I see a girl who's usually strong and willful crying when she's alone."

That sounded pretty specific for just an example. Akutagawa's heart must have been touched by the tears of a strong-willed girl who seemed like she would never cry.

I suddenly recalled the vulnerability Kotobuki had shown when she was in the hospital.

She was always cold, so when her head was downcast and tears had filled her eyes, I'd been shaken. When I remembered the way she had looked in that moment, it made me a little nervous.

I doubted that Akutagawa had fallen for Kotobuki or anything like that, though.

But wait — Akutagawa's girlfriend Sarashina wasn't the strong, stubborn type, was she? Or maybe she looked quiet but was actually rambunctious like Tohko? If all you did was look at her, you would think Tohko was just a demure book girl, after all.

"And you? What's your type?"

When he asked the question so suddenly, I was stuck for an answer.

There was no way I was going to open up about the dear girl I missed so much, who floated through my mind like a phantom. My chest felt like it was going to rip open.

"No clue," I muttered, forcing a smile.

I hadn't noticed the air growing dark and chilly, and our inky shadows bobbed across the lamp-lit asphalt. We started discussing harmless topics and then went our separate ways.

⊰◈⊱

How many letters have I sent you now?

I got emotional in the letter I sent the other day and wrote some harsh things, which I regret.

I had forgotten that even now you're in the midst of a long, painful battle. It must feel like everything in the world is out to get you, like everything is coming at you with weapons drawn. Over and over you were betrayed, you were hurt, and even your last wish was disrupted by the person closest to you. So you may firmly believe that you have not a single ally in the world.

Your indomitable will, your burning spirit — they come from your hatred and refusal of the world. I understand that now. And that the way you are now, that very hatred is a crutch you need to keep yourself standing.

But even so, I will not tolerate you turning your hateful looks on me. I wish to be your protector so greatly that it threatens to crack my heart. You may not believe me when I say that I *have* avoided seeing you. But I truly want to be a friend to you.

If you didn't wish any dishonorable acts of me, I believe I would run joyously to your side.

So I wish you would be calm. I wish you would open your heart, just a little bit.

If I told you that I couldn't sleep for fear that you might be crying, you would probably get angry and slap me.

Chapter 2 – Lemon Cookies Taste of Youth

Several days after deciding on the casting, I was in the club room, beginning to focus on writing the script.

"Mushanokōji's novels are composed of dialogue and the main character's soliloquy-like exposition, so it should be easy to turn into a script. If anyone can do it, it's you, Konoha. I believe in you!"

Tohko smiled, but just because there was a bit of dialogue, that didn't mean I could just copy and paste it into the script. And there weren't enough actors, so Sugiko's brother Nakata and his friends couldn't be in it. I had to massage their lines, so they wouldn't sound unnatural, and we couldn't change locations whenever we wanted. And long lines might work in a novel, but if a line went on too long onstage, it would be awkward and bore the audience.

Peering back and forth between my notebooks and the copy of *Friendship* I'd taken out of the library, I wrestled the sentences out with a look of agony on my face while Tohko sat beside me indelicately with her feet up on her fold-up chair, reveling in giving orders.

"Write it so it communicates Omiya's hidden feelings and

Sugiko's passion for him to the audience. The bittersweet triangle between Nojima, Omiya, and Sugiko is the tastiest part of this story.

"Nojima is lost in a joyous fantasy at being in love with someone, and Omiya discreetly supports his friend, all while being tempted by Sugiko — oh, it's so romantic!

"Omiya treats Sugiko coldly on purpose, but she only starts to like him more and more because of it. Sugiko is adorable in the scene where she and her friend Takeko are playing cards with Nojima and Omiya, and she's so uncomfortable that she blushes and spaces out and messes things up.

"Yes — it's steamy and warms the inside of your mouth and stomach like simmered tofu, but sprinkled with ponzu sauce made from squeezed citrus. You sympathize with Nojima's feelings at the same time, and the faint whiffs of tart citrus prick your heart.

"You gotta make the friendship between Nojima and Omiya really rich, too. Nanase mentioned this part, too, but when Sugiko is about to go abroad and Nojima comes to the station to see her off and tells her, 'I hope you'll be happy,' while fighting back his feelings for her? That scene is so moving. It hurts a little, like when you almost burn your tongue on hot tofu.

"Some think that Omiya is based on Mushanokōji's fellow White Birch author, Naoya Shiga. Mushanokōji, who had to live a frugal life despite coming from the nobility, and Shiga, the son of a wealthy family who greatly enjoyed his life as a student. Mushanokōji was bad at sports, and Shiga was a well-rounded athlete. These two different people who grew up in such similar environments and had such similar personalities became the best of friends through their creative work. They would even go on trips together on foot. They were good friends their whooole lives, even after they got old."

While Tohko was eagerly relating episodes from Mushanokōji

and Shiga's friendship, she grabbed sheets of discarded paper, tearing them up and munching on them.

"Hmmm. I think the lines are a little too long and that's watering down the taste. Rhythm is the lifeblood of dialogue. The important lines need a calm, unhurried beat, like you're chopping up a carrot with a kitchen knife. The comic scenes move the knife with a short, quick beat. Bam-bam-*bam!*

"Oh! This part is fantastic! It's like perfectly chilled tofu sliding down my throat. This is it! This is the taste of Mushanokōji."

"Ugh. This part is *sooo* tough. There's a burned-up shrimp tail inside my tofuuu!

"Ooh, this part is so warm and tasty! It's like I took a bite and have to blow on it before I can swallow. Konoha, you're a genius!"

Dropping parts and picking others up, she crinkled and crunched through the script I'd written.

"Why are you eating the parts that I balled up and threw away? It's going to give you diarrhea."

She lifted her long lashes just a touch at that, dyed in the honey-colored light of the western sun that shone through the window, and her lips curved into a smile.

"No, it won't. Your snacks have toughened me up, so my stomach's not gonna be bested by these little scraps of nothing. Besides, they're simple and delicious — like getting the crusts of bread from a bakery, maybe? And eeevery once in a while, there's a smudge of strawberry or blueberry jam still on them, and then I feel like I hit the jackpot."

I was aghast at how truly insatiable Tohko could be when it came to "food." But I got a strange ticklish sensation deep in my chest as I watched her carefully smooth out the messed-up pages, tear them up with her slender fingers, and then bring them eagerly to her lips.

"So how has Akutagawa been since we talked to him?" Tohko asked around a piece of paper in her mouth.

"Nothing out of the ordinary. Same as ever."

After that day we went home together, I hadn't had any deep conversations with him. The more I tried to find out about him, the less I could hide about myself. About my past, about who I used to like, about what had happened to her. I didn't want anyone to know about that.

I told Sarashina that I was sorry, but I couldn't get anything out of him. I felt a little guilty meeting someone else's girlfriend alone in an empty hallway during a break.

When Sarashina found out that Akutagawa was going to be in a play for the culture fair, she seemed shocked.

"You said...Kazushi is going to be in your play? Really?" she had murmured in her frail voice, her head drooping as tears gathered in her eyes.

As Tohko chomped on the script, she mumbled, "You don't have many friends, Konoha. You should treasure Akutagawa."

That word sent a sharp chill through my very core.

Were we friends? Akutagawa and me?

Sure, we shared our notes from class and talked to each other, but...we weren't like Nojima and Omiya, discussing our futures or getting advice on love or experiencing such strong friendship that it brought us to tears, and we had never wanted to do everything in our power to help the other.

The bond between Nojima and Omiya was strong and beautiful. But then, if they hadn't been such good friends that they shared their every thought, Omiya would never have suffered so much for loving Sugiko, and Nojima could have avoided being hurt by Omiya's betrayal.

Yeah — if they hadn't expected anything from others or opened up so much, then they wouldn't have lost anything or been disappointed...

That was why I would never trust anyone or love the way Nojima had.

"I'm so glad Akutagawa agreed to perform. Wouldn't it be great if everyone loved the play and our membership went up?"

Hugging her knees on the fold-up chair in the twilight, Tohko's eyes crinkled up with an easy smile.

"If that happens, you won't be able to graze anymore."

"Oh no! You're right. But I also want a ton of members. I mean, the future of the club is…But, but, but — I want to eat my *snacks* — augh! I don't know!"

The sight of her sulking like a little kid in her deep, almost tearful conflict warmed my heart just a little.

That weekend, I continued writing at home.

Around noon on Sunday, I was zoning out, buried in masses of paper, when there was a knock on my door and my mother came in.

"Konoha? Come down, we're having lunch soon. Hmm?"

When she saw the tall stack of papers on my desk, her eyes went wide. I hurried to explain.

"I'm writing an essay for homework. It's really hard. I messed up all that paper."

My mother smiled at me kindly.

"Such a trooper. But your spaghetti's going to get soggy. Hurry up."

Once she'd closed the door and I was alone again, I couldn't help but notice that my cheeks were burning. Had my mother realized that I'd lied to her?

I could have just told her that I was writing the script for a play for the culture fair. It wouldn't have been a big deal.

My family knows I'm in the book club at school.

But I hadn't told them that until almost two months after I'd joined, and I explained that, "We don't have many members, so we don't sponsor any big activities. I just sit around and talk about books with Tohko." But I didn't mention that Tohko had me writing improv stories for her every day.

I didn't want to make my family worry unnecessarily…

Two years earlier, when I was still in middle school, I submitted the first novel I ever wrote to a magazine's new author competition, and for some reason I was selected for the grand prize — the youngest winner in history.

After that, my life turned upside down. I was marketed everywhere as a mysterious young girl, my prizewinning novel became a best seller, and the name Miu Inoue became renowned throughout Japan.

But it brought me nothing but misfortune and cast me headlong into deepest darkness. I lost the girl that I loved, suffered from fits where I suddenly couldn't breathe, became a shut-in who ditched school, and caused my family a ton of problems.

Even now, my mother worried because I never went out with other people on my days off and never got phone calls from friends. Sometimes she would look at me sadly.

At those times, when memories of the past mounted unexpectedly in my heart, I felt like my life was sad and impotent, and my throat tightened.

Why am I so weak? Will I keep dragging this out forever?

I don't want to break anything or lose anything ever again. That was why I decided I would never write another novel. I had been wrong to think about writing a novel back in middle school.

I closed my notebook and went downstairs in a funk with Nojima's lines sticking in my mind:

"Precious, precious girl.

"I will be a man worthy of becoming your husband.

"Until I am, I beg you not to marry another."

Like Nojima, I, too, had been in love and oblivious to everything else. But I would never see that girl again.

I had typed up and printed out clean copies of the script. When I handed them over on Monday morning in the book club room, Tohko's face twisted, and she shouted at me, practically sobbing.

"Noooooo! Why didn't you write it by hand?! When each letter is written down on pure white paper in pencil, it's like homemade rice and it's sooo yummy. You know how much I like handwriting! This is so mean! Just — so mean!"

"If I handwrote a script on lined paper, it would be too hard to read. And you would just end up eating it."

"I — I would not. Hmmph. So you know how to use a computer, huh?"

"Necessity compelled me to learn. Doesn't everyone know how nowadays? I can even type without looking at the keyboard."

"Traitor."

She glared at me tearfully, but then suddenly her face brightened and she stretched both her hands out at me. "Oh, right! You must have a handwritten first draft! Hand it over."

"The paper recycling was this morning, so I tied it up with some comics and put it out on the curb."

"How *cruel!!* How could you do that?! Ogre — demon — president taunter!" Tohko wept.

"Can you get some bound copies made?" I replied heartlessly. "Here's a copy of the file."

I tried to hand her a CD and leave, but Tohko grabbed the cuff of my sleeve, her face an angry pout.

"Hold on a minute, Konoha. You're going to pay for this. I have an important mission for you now. Since I'm such a benevolent mentor, I'll forgive you for the whole script thing if you pull this off."

Geez. How blatantly was she going to keep using me?

At lunch, already in a state of resignation, I visited the orchestra.

Inside the grand building that rose up on our campus was a vast main hall and several smaller auditoriums and other little rooms, and on the top floor was the workroom of the orchestra's club president, the third-year girl who served as its conductor, Maki Himekura — alias "the Princess."

"Excuse me."

I pushed open the door and went into the studio. It was filled with light, and at its center, Maki, a sturdy-looking girl, swept her brush over a canvas. Her sleeves were rolled up, and she wore a work apron over her school uniform.

Watercolors and sketches decorated the walls, and there was an expensive-looking mahogany bookshelf that contained gorgeous rows of luxuriously bound volumes of literature.

"Come in, Konoha."

Maki hitched her sensuous lips up in a smile. Her wavy, light brown hair poured over her chest and back like a lion's mane, shining golden in the light.

"Are you delivering a message for Tohko today? Sit, have some tea. Relax."

With polished movements, a tall man dressed in a black suit set out sandwiches, fruit, and cups of tea on a small table covered with a tablecloth.

His name was Takamizawa, and he worked under Maki's grandfather, the school's director. That was why Maki was called "the Princess" and why she received so many special privileges at school.

To be honest, I didn't like her very much. Probably because I was an herbivore and she was a carnivore. I felt that if I let my guard down, her sharp fangs and claws would tear me apart.

"Thank you."

I drank some tea at her urging and picked up a sandwich. The sandwich was very good—salmon and cucumbers between thinly sliced bread with just the right amount of salt—but perhaps due to the presence of a threat right in front of me, I found it difficult to swallow.

"You know, lately whenever Tohko sees me, she gets in a huff and runs off. Do you suppose she hates me?" Maki asked, though it sounded like she enjoyed getting a reaction like that out of Tohko.

"It's because you keep pressuring her to pose nude for you."

"You think? But I fell in love with her the moment I saw her. There aren't many subjects like that. I'd love to talk her into it somehow before we graduate. You'd want to see her nude portrait, too, wouldn't you, Konoha?"

"Not interested. I don't need to see Tohko's chest. I'm used to seeing my own in the mirror."

"So then, you'd rather see me naked?"

I spit out my tea. Maki gave me a slow smile. "Joking."

"Please, don't do that. It's bad for my nerves."

"Don't tell Tohko. It will only make her hate me more."

"I think talking like that is what made her hate you. And because you taunt her about how few members the book club has and how small our room is and how it's like we don't even exist on campus."

"But Tohko is so adorable when she's enraged. I love it."

This wasn't going to work. Maki had no desire to reform. I would just do what I came here to do and then leave. Otherwise, I was afraid she might devour me at any second.

"Tohko only gets so infuriated because you rile her up like that, and then all the problems start. You should take some responsibility."

Maki grinned.

"I heard that you're doing a play for the culture fair? You seem to have secured your players, but you can't rehearse in that tiny room of yours. You need lighting and sets, too, don't you?"

She seemed to know perfectly well why I had been conscripted to come here. Clumsy tricks weren't going to work on her.

"Yes. And we don't have many alums and no influence or connections, so we're stuck. Would you consider helping us out?"

I took several photos out of the pocket of my uniform and arranged them on the table.

A smile made Maki's eyes narrow.

"Looks like you've gotten much better at bargaining than the last time you tried to threaten me."

One picture showed Tohko in her P.E. clothes failing to catch a volleyball and toppling to the ground. Another showed her in a swimsuit stretched out next to the pool while blubbering over a cramped leg. A boy from the photography club had sold the pictures to me, and I'd held onto them thinking they might be useful to quiet Tohko down whenever she ran amok. I never thought I'd end up putting them to use like this.

Maki traced the lines of Tohko's body. The way she moved her finger was a little obscene.

"But you're still too green."

"Huh?"

"I've got hundreds of photos capturing Tohko's activities at school that are cuter and taken at much greater risk than these."

"H-hundreds?"

"If you want to barter with photos, go find something more unusual. Even better, a nude of Tohko or a private photo."

"That's...criminal."

Maki chuckled.

"Fine. I'll accept these. You can use an empty hall to practice in, and I'll take care of the lighting and everything."

"Are you sure?"

I looked at her uncertainly. Considering who I was dealing with, there had to be something more to this.

"Ha. I wouldn't miss Tohko's performance. You're doing Saneatsu Mushanokōji, aren't you? I wouldn't mind adding a picture of Tohko in fluttering kimono sleeves and unbraided hair to my collection."

I decided to stay quiet about Tohko playing a man's role.

"Thank you. I know this is going to make Tohko happy, too."

I bowed my head meekly and left the room.

"You did it, Konoha. You really are my apprentice! I always believed in you."

Tohko had been waiting for me outside and started heaping praise on me as soon as she heard the news.

What an act. She just didn't want to ask Maki for a favor herself, so she sent me to do it.

"This solves all our problems. We'll start rehearsals as soon as school's over!"

"Wooow, this script is so warm! Look, Nanase!"

"Don't shove it in my face, Takeda. But wow! It really is."

"Heh-heh. It's fresh out of the oven and piping hot."

After school, we gathered in the small auditorium that Maki had provided for us. There were fifty seats upholstered in red cloth, in front of which was a small half-circular stage about the height of a podium. It was the perfect environment in which to rehearse. I went around passing out the freshly printed scripts to everyone, and we started reading.

"I believe I may once have seen a photograph of her myself at my cousin's home. She was quite beautiful."

Surprisingly, Akutagawa gave a flawless performance as Omiya.

It was probably partially due to the fact that his deep voice gave a sense of stoicism and honor that matched the role, but he also read off the old-fashioned lines serenely without stumbling.

On the other hand, our lead actor Tohko...

"'Quite beautiful' hardly begins to describe her!"

Hmmmmm. Your voice sounds a little too forced, Tohko... She seemed to be trying deliberately to sound like a man, but her voice was smarmy, like a lady-killer with a rose in his mouth.

Plus her slightest movement was exaggerated, and each time she said something, she spread her arms wide or lifted them up or arched them back or hugged them around her head and moaned. Next to Akutagawa's restrained performance, hers was too unbalanced and felt totally out of place.

"Storms rage through this world: storms of ideology. I rise up in the midst of them like a single great tree and yield not one step to their tempests. Sugiko is the one who grants me that strength. The fact that she believes in me."

She writhed around, rocking her body from side to side like a tree swaying in the wind; then she changed it up and clasped her hands in front of her chest, batted her eyelashes exaggeratedly, and said in a coquettish, saccharine voice, "Ohhh, Mister *Nojima*! I do believe in you, you dear man. You will be victorious. *Please,* make me your *wife!*"

"Cut! Cut!"

I leaped in front of Tohko after this erratic performance, unable to take any more.

"What is it, Hayakawa? I would appreciate it if you didn't inter-fere with Sugiko and I while we discuss our love."

"I'm not Hayakawa! I don't care if this scene *is* all in Nojima's imagination, it's just creepy when you emphasize every other word like *'Please,* make me your *wife.'* You need to cut it out. I don't remember writing all those italics in the script. And your movements are way too exaggerated, too."

"I just got too into the role, and my mouth and body started moving without me. I must have some talent as an actress to become such a completely different person."

"What you were doing just then only counts as a crazy person."

"Whaaaat? I was trying to act out the despondency and naïveté of a young man in love, but still give a little wink to the audience."

"If it's too despondent, it looks vacant. Don't add in extra action. Play it more ordinary."

"But then Nojima's feelings won't come across to the audience!"

"If it comes across too much, everyone's just embarrassed for you!"

Kotobuki watched wide-eyed as Tohko and I talked. Akutagawa looked surprised, too. I realized that I was cutting in on Tohko like I usually did, and I caught myself.

"A-anyway, can you just follow the script?"

Tohko gave a noncommittal answer—"Uh-huh"—and then went back to practicing. What was wrong with me? I was passing as a friendly, quiet guy in class and everything.

"Sugiko, Sugiko. Look at that cloud. It looks like someone, do you not think?"

"Who, I wonder?"

Takeda was good, too. Even though her role was as a dignified girl the exact opposite of who she normally was, she sounded just right.

Kotobuki must have been nervous, because her performance was stiff. She looked embarrassed when she was saying her lines. Maybe she was more shy than she looked. When our eyes met, she flushed and hurriedly looked away.

"Konoha — it's your line, Konoha."

"Oh — right. 'Ha-ha-ha! God forbid, I encounter Takeko.' "

"Geez, Konoha, you sound so wooden."

"Your laugh is pretty fake, Inoue."

"Konohaaa, try to put a little more *feeling* into it!"

... (Silence.)

My Hayakawa got panned.

After rehearsal was over, Takeda went over to Tohko.

"Tooohko? There's a store opening next to the station today. They gave me a flyer, and they have this cute stationery stuff that doesn't cost too much. Do you want to come with me?"

"Why not! What about you, Nanase?"

"I don't really... Well, if Tohko's going..."

"Yaaay! Nanase's coming toooo!"

At first they had been awkward together, but in their own way Kotobuki and Takeda seemed to be getting along. Once the three girls had gone, Akutagawa and I left the auditorium.

Bathed in the same red light of the setting sun as on that other day, Akutagawa pushed his bike and I walked beside him.

"Man, acting is hard."

"Don't worry about it. You're not a professional actor, so of course, you're not going to be great at it."

"But you were awesome, Akutagawa. You projected your voice and everything. I was surprised."

"Really? All I did was read the script, though."

"Well, your real voice is great to begin with. Omiya really is the perfect role for you."

"...I suppose so."

Huh? That sounded dark. I was trying to praise him, but maybe I'd said something wrong.

And just then, Akutagawa's eyes widened in surprise.

At the other end of the slowly darkening campus, an old cherry tree grew next to the school gate, rising up red and black in the sunset. Its darkly tinged leaves and gnarled branches fanned out drearily. Half hidden behind it stood Sarashina.

Her sorrowful eyes were full of tears, and her limbs and lips trembled, as if it was the middle of winter.

Sarashina suddenly ran at us and threw herself against Akutagawa's chest, then brokenly begged, "Kazushi...what...should I do? Help me...Kazushi —"

Something cold shot down my spine. Sarashina's fingers clutching at Akutagawa's jacket — I saw they were covered in a red liquid.

Blood? Or was it only the light of the setting sun?

As sobs racked her body, Akutagawa wrapped his arms around her as if to hide her. He bowed his head over her, his face twisted in pain.

The next day, I spotted Akutagawa on the way to school.

He stopped his bike and dropped a long white envelope into a mailbox.

The moment I saw how tense his face was, I thought back to what had happened the day before.

I wasn't sure whether I should call out to him, but then he looked in my direction and our eyes met.

"Morning."

I gave him a slight smile, and after a moment's hesitation showing on his face, he gave the same smile back.

"Morning, Inoue."

Pushing down the thrumming anxiety in my heart, I walked over to him.

"I saw you sending a letter before, too."

"My parents asked me to. Insurance forms or something."

We continued talking about harmless subjects as we walked alongside each other.

After we'd gone through the school gate, Akutagawa suddenly muttered in a low voice, "Sorry about yesterday."

My heart skipped. I'd left the two of them alone after Sarashina had appeared and gone home by myself, so I didn't know what they had talked about. Or why she had been crying. Or the true nature of the stuff glistening on the tips of her slender fingers...

"Was that girl your girlfriend?" I asked, pretending I didn't know who Sarashina was.

Akutagawa knit his brow and answered with some difficulty, "...Not anymore."

"So you two used to go out?"

"...Yeah."

What? Sarashina had made it sound like they were still dating...

"Sorry. I can't say anything else. It gets into her business."

The creases on Akutagawa's forehead deepened, and he pressed his mouth into a line. For some reason, my heart started to ache.

"No, I'm sorry. I won't ask about it. Actually, my English homework..."

I changed the subject in my usual tone of voice.

After class, we rehearsed in the small auditorium.

I'd said I wouldn't ask anything else, but I kept wondering what had happened between Akutagawa and Sarashina.

Akutagawa was intrepidly performing onstage as Omiya. It was the scene where he and Tohko as Nojima had their discussion about love.

"If a person is granted that extraordinary emotion called love, we have no right to mock it."

I mulled things over in my mind. It could be that Akutagawa felt that they had broken up, but she didn't. Maybe there was someone else that Akutagawa liked.

"At the very least, the Japanese are far too disdainful of love. Not you, Nakata, but they regard it as safer to give their daughters not to a man who loves them, but rather to a total stranger."

And was it really my imagination that made it look like Sarashina's fingers had been colored red?

"Sorry! I need a bathroom break real quick."

Takeda pattered off between the seats, and we took a break.

Tohko walked over to Akutagawa with a smile.

"Do you have a second? It's about the scene where Nojima's book got lambasted and Omiya calms him down. If you take a longer pause at the line where you say, 'Your revenge is in the offing. I doubt there's anyone with less cause to be dejected than you,' I think it'll have more of an impact on the audience. 'In the offing' is referring to the future, right? You'll have your revenge in the future, meaning, 'there's no doubt that you're going to succeed eventually, and the price for that is that you have to suffer ill luck now.' So Omiya is applauding Nojima. This is a particularly delicious scene where we can sense the type of man Omiya is and his friendship with Nojima, so don't let it just flow by. Let's make it stick a little more. I'll express how touched I am with my entire body. Right, like imagine it's —"

It sounded like they were hammering out a strategy for the play, and Akutagawa nodded attentively. It was the polar opposite of how I always let Tohko's words wash over me.

I sat in a seat, and when I stole a glance over, I saw Kotobuki had come to sit beside me. She whispered, "Hey...do you think Akutagawa likes Tohko?"

"Huh? Y-you think?"

Akutagawa and Tohko? No way. If anything, wasn't Tohko the one vying for his attention? Well, not that I cared either way...

Then Kotobuki leaned forward and stuck out her lip, grumbling, "I mean, isn't it weird that Akutagawa would be in this play? When his class put on a play for the culture fair last year, all the girls wanted him to play the lead! But he told them he couldn't act. That's what my friend Mori told me. She was in his class last year, and she was really disappointed."

"What was their play about?"

"It was *Swan Lake*. Akutagawa would have been Siegfried."

"Er, you sure he just didn't want that role?"

I sure wouldn't want to dress up like a prince now that I was in high school.

"But the girl who played Odette was the prettiest girl in their class. A girl named Sarashina."

My heart skipped.

Did she say Sarashina? They'd been in the same class? So that was why Sarashina had looked so gloomy when she heard Akutagawa was going to be in our play.

Kotobuki lowered her voice and continued in a whisper, "It's bizarre that he would kick aside a role opposite someone like Sarashina, who's so popular with all the boys, and then go and act in the book club's play. But if Akutagawa had a thing for Tohko, I could see it."

When Kotobuki said that, she stole a glance up at me through her eyelashes.

Wellll…the reason Akutagawa agreed to do it was because he owed Tohko. But I couldn't tell her that.

Then Kotobuki became timid all of a sudden.

"But I forgot, Tohko has a boyfriend. So there's no hope, I guess."

Did I just hear that?

"What are you talking about?"

Tohko had a boyfriend?! Could she actually get a boyfriend?! What kind of freak was he?!

"It — it's true. She told me herself. Her boyfriend is this great guy who looks really good in a white scarf. He's hunting bears in Hokkaido so she never gets to see him and she's lonely, but he just sent her some salted salmon he caught and she said it was really good. She'd probably never even notice a boy from school."

A white scarf?

Hunting bears?

Salmon?

When I lined the words up like prompts for an improv story, I remembered Tohko telling me with deadly seriousness about an old woman she met in Shin — who had told her fortune and informed her she was inside a zone of romantic slaughter.

And that the summer her zone of romantic slaughter dissipated, she would fall into a fated love with a man wearing a white scarf in front of a bear with a salmon in its mouth...

In my mind, I could see an image of the young man in the white scarf hurling a spear at the bear with the salmon in its mouth. I felt dizzy and ready to collapse into my seat. No, Kotobuki — Tohko was just trying to sound important.

Kotobuki kept talking quickly, her words sounding frantic.

"So, uh, Akutagawa might get dumped. Tohko has a boyfriend and all. There's no point in falling for her. Don't you feel awful? F-for Akutagawa, I mean."

I listened to her talk with a grave look, my shoulders slumped.

———⋙◈⋘———

I'm going to appear in the book club's play at the culture fair.

The play is Mushanokōji's *Friendship*. Have you ever read it?

My role is a man named Omiya, who falls for the woman his best friend loves. In the end, he steals the woman from his friend. When I was reading the script, I couldn't help seeing my past and present selves in him.

I'm also an awful person who betrayed someone who trusted me.

No matter how much I regret it, I will never be able to erase the mistakes of that day.

How many nights did I have nightmares that the classroom was dyed in a sea of blood as a girl with long hair and a chisel stuck in her chest collapsed, blood flowing from her body? How often did I hear her voice berating me for breaking my promise? Each time, I repeated my penance, jolting awake and shuddering at the sensation of the sweat that poured off me cooling on my skin.

Ever since that day when my shameful choice brought down the worst results and hurt people, I've tried hard to pretend to be a person of integrity, but in the end I'm repeating the same mistake over again.

I meant to make the best choices wisely and cautiously, but yet again I was ruining the lives of the people who had placed their trust in me, causing them pain and sorrow.

What did I do wrong?

When did it happen? Where?

Perhaps, as foolish as I am, I have no capacity to protect you. Six years ago, I was trying to protect my friend. Even if it was a betrayal to my friend, I believed I would save her by doing it. But that was an error based on ignorance.

And I cannot shake from my mind the thought that I am even now making a mistake. I am afraid of granting your wish, because there's no guarantee at all that it's the right thing to do.

But what will become of you the moment I turn my back? When I consider that, doubt smolders in my heart as it has always done over whether it's the right choice to go to you and comply with your wish — whether or not you insult me or despise me.

But no. It would be dishonorable.

I hope that you read this letter instead of destroying it.

<hr>

Two whole weeks went by.

There was no marked change in Akutagawa's behavior after all that, so I thought he must have solved his problem with Sarashina.

That day after school, everyone rehearsed the play again.

"They say those who have truly loved will never be broken-hearted. That seems so sad, almost unbearably sad."

Akutagawa was giving a good performance, of course. The words he spoke so smoothly felt fringed with pain and melancholy. Maybe that was because he was going through a painful romance right now.

On the other hand, Tohko's Nojima continued to be high-strung. It looked like she had already memorized her lines; she didn't need to look at the script and could throw herself into the role, overacting like a mustache-twirling foreigner.

"Nakata, you say that love is like painting a picture on cloth, but I think not. That pays too little credit to the other person."

In the pauses between lines, she strained, saying "hnnngh" and "urgggh," and I wished she would stop.

Even in the scene where they played Ping-Pong at Sugiko's house, Tohko acted creepy.

There were two Ping-Pong scenes, one where Nojima goes to visit Sugiko's house and they have fun playing, though Sugiko is going easy on him. The other was when her brother and his friends gather at her house for a Ping-Pong tournament, and

Sugiko crushes her opponents one after the other, awash in applause, until Omiya takes her down with his merciless play. The two scenes are important for contrasting Nojima and Omiya.

Since there was no way we could hit a real ball, we decided to just pretend and play a sound effect for the actual show.

As Tohko waved her paddle around, she laughed boisterously, "Ah-ha-ha-ha!

"I'm playing Ping-Pong with Sugiko! Sugiko is infinitely better at Ping-Pong than I. But she did nothing to intimidate me. Instead she was kind to me and passed me easy balls that were child's play for me to return. It was impossible not to sense Sugiko's character in that."

She swung the paddle up high and shouted, "Ha!

"Where else would I find a woman so innocent, beautiful, and pure, so considerate and so lovely? God is offering this woman to me. How cruel He would be otherwise."

Tohko's spirited performance was drawing Kotobuki as Sugiko out a little.

"You're quite good, Mister Nojima."

This turn-of-the-century story of adolescence flush with romance became a comedy every time Tohko opened her mouth. The famous scenes I had worked so hard on were like skits for a variety show, and I was incredibly nervous about the live performance.

When it was break time, Kotobuki removed the lid of a pink lunch box and held it out for Tohko, fidgeting all the while.

"Um — I baked some cookies. Help yourselves."

Paper napkins with a cute flower pattern were spread out inside the lunch box, which was stuffed with adorable cookies topped with things like almonds or blueberry jam.

"Whoa! You *made* these, Nanase? That's amazing! They're great!"

"Thanks, Nanase. Let's all try one."

Tohko couldn't taste anything but words. She'd told me before that food had no flavor, like if you or I were to eat paper. Wasn't this gross for her?

I watched, panicked, as she reached straight into the box, grabbed a round cookie topped with an almond, and put it into her mouth.

A bright smile spread over Tohko's face as she chewed.

"Yummm! The fragrance of the almond and the vanilla aroma melt together exquisitely in my mouth to produce an airy harmony."

"Oh, don't exaggerate, Tohko!"

Kotobuki turned red as a flame.

"But it really is delicious, Nanase! It's a restrained sweetness, so even boys would be totally okay eating these."

Takeda beamed as she ate her cookie, too. Kotobuki's cheeks burned even brighter at that, and her voice squeaked when she next spoke, stealing a glance at me.

"I — I'm on a diet. Right now. So I thought I'd try reducing the sugar. That's all."

Until then, all my attention had been on Tohko.

"Oh, let me get one."

I hurriedly grabbed a leaf-shaped cookie and took a bite. There was a firm, homemade texture, but at the same time an unexpectedly tart taste spread over my tongue. Was this lemon?

"Yeah, they're really good, Kotobuki," I said.

Kotobuki looked away, stumbling over her words. "O-oh? I wasn't thinking about what you'd like when I made them, obviously."

Tohko gobbled up cookie after cookie, chattering like a bird.

"This one's blueberry, isn't it? The jam makes a great accent! I can feel the sweet jam melting over my tongue! Hmm, what's this brown one?"

"Cocoa and nuts."

"Oh! Cocoa! This is cocoa, of course! There's a tiny hint of bitterness, but then the crisp sweetness of the nuts joins in. It's incredible."

"You sound like a pastry critic, Tohko!"

"Oh yes, I love sweet things!"

Tohko was chucking so many cookies into her mouth and describing her impressions of each one so that I was hanging in suspense.

She was better off stopping while she was still ahead. She was going to slip up if she got too carried away. And besides, could her stomach take being crammed with all that tasteless stuff? If we ate paper, there was no question it would mess up our stomachs. Wouldn't the opposite be true for Tohko?

"Oh, man, these leaf-shaped cookies are *so* sweet! Yum!"

"What? It's sweet?" Kotobuki got a strange look on her face. "That's a lemon cookie. It's pretty tart."

Uh-oh — you blew it.

Tohko made a quick excuse. "Oh — oh no, you're right. Looks like that was the only part that was sweet. Yeah, it's tart, but ever so slightly sweet, like youth."

Somehow or other, she seemed to have recovered, and I relaxed.

Just then, I noticed Akutagawa looking down into the box of cookies with a critical eye.

His expression was pained, as if he saw something he didn't want to see.

A chill ran through my heart.

"Is something wrong, Akutagawa?"

My question seemed to hit him physically, then a complicated smile came over his face. "No, it's nothing."

He took a cocoa-flavored cookie and ate it.

"I'm not a big fan of sweet things, but even I can eat these. They taste good," he said.

Was that dark look he'd had just now because he didn't like sweet things? I didn't think that was all it was, and something stirred deep inside me.

Akutagawa reached for another cookie. When he'd eaten the next one, he got another—he continued eating steadily with a detached look on his face. That stirred up even more anxiety in me. It seemed like he was forcing himself to eat something he didn't want to eat.

On the other hand, Tohko popped cookies into her mouth with a sunny smile.

Akutagawa and Tohko—did either of them really enjoy what they were eating?

Tohko's tongue at least wasn't detecting anything, no matter how sweet it was. She wasn't capable of tasting.

When Tohko reached for the very last leaf-shaped lemon cookie, I shot my hand out and grabbed her arm.

"You've had a lot, Tohko. I want this one."

Tohko's eyes widened.

I picked up the last cookie and put it in my mouth.

Akutagawa and Takeda looked at me with surprise on their faces.

Kotobuki gaped at me, her face bright red, as I gulped down the cookie.

Silence filled the stage.

"Uh—um, because…because these cookies are really good!" I offered quickly in my defense when I realized how that had looked. Kotobuki rolled her eyes.

"D-don't be stupid. You think it makes me happy to hear you complimenting me?"

"Ooooh, you're blushing, Nanase."

"Shut it, Takeda."

Kotobuki glared at Takeda, her face bright red. Takeda giggled. My cheeks were burning, too. Geez, what was I doing?

"Um—practice! Let's practice!" someone shouted. But just then, the pocket of Akutagawa's pants vibrated.

Akutagawa was startled and looked down at his pocket. He took out his cell phone and looked at the screen, and then his face became even more tense.

"Sorry. I have to go do something, so I need to leave early."

He ducked his head, then slung his bag over his shoulder and left.

"I wonder what that was about."

The three girls looked puzzled. I also wondered who had been on the other end of the line. Could it have been Sarashina?

But rehearsal quickly started back up, and I had to play Omiya for Akutagawa.

In the scenes where Omiya and Sugiko shared lines, Kotobuki tripped up several times, and she would complain, her cheeks flushing, "You're really bad at this, Inoue. This is so hard."

That evening, when rehearsals were over, Tohko rushed out, saying she had forgotten to record the cooking segment of some news show or other.

Takeda also waved and bounded off with a "See you tomorrow, guysss!" leaving Kotobuki and me by ourselves.

Once I'd packed up my script and notebook, my eyes met Kotobuki's. She had already finished getting her stuff together and was standing around, looking out of place.

"Huh? Aren't you going home, Kotobuki?"

"Yes," she snapped, then immediately looked away in embarrassment. "Um...you think I should make more cookies?"

"Huh?"

"It looked like you wanted more."

"Yeah, they were really good. But doesn't it take a lot of time? I wouldn't want to trouble you."

"N-not at all. I actually kind of like cooking. Although you probably think I don't look like the type who would. Plus Tohko seemed to like them."

"Yes, well…"

See, Tohko? This is what happens when you gobble up cookies you can't taste and pretend that they're delicious. Geez, now what? Maybe I'd make Tohko eat all the cookies she couldn't taste. It would only be what she deserved. Or…?

I was still thinking it over when Kotobuki's face turned suddenly indifferent.

"So it was just flattery after all."

"Wha — no!"

"That's the kind of guy you are, Inoue. You'll be nice and smiley for anyone, but deep inside they have no idea what you're thinking."

I felt a chill, as if I'd been stabbed in the chest with an icicle.

"Never mind. Jerk."

Kotobuki slung her bag (from which dangled a pink rabbit doll) over her shoulder, bit down hard on her lip, and hastily left the room.

I'd made her mad…again. Why did things always go that way with her?

The word *jerk* played on a loop in my mind, putting me into a sullen mood, when I heard a sigh.

"Poor Nanase. I didn't think you were that dense, Konoha."

Takeda stuck her head inside the door, and I thought my heart was going to stop. I thought she'd already left.

She walked toward me, her face a carefree mask.

"I forgot something, but things were looking pretty promising and I didn't want to interrupt, so I stayed outside."

"You mean you spied on us."

"Or you could call it that."

She grinned toothily, then bent over the seats and picked up a binder she'd left there.

"Nanase is *pretty* straightforward. Really, she puts up such a huge front it ticks me off and makes me want to tease her, but I wonder how come you can't see it. Didn't you see the pink rabbit on her bag?"

I cocked my head to one side.

"I saw the rabbit, but so what? Oh — you don't think Kotobuki likes Akutagawa, do you?"

Kotobuki had seemed pretty concerned about Tohko and him, so I thought it might be possible. But Takeda's shoulders slumped magnificently and she sighed.

"This is what I mean. This is why Nanase calls you a jerk. Whatever. Just act all flustered later. You're cute when you do that."

"Wait, what? Can you be a little clearer?"

"Nope. It's a secret."

Takeda hugged the binder to her chest and giggled. There was a white angel's wing stretching across the dandelion-colored plastic.

I gasped. "That binder!"

"Heh-heh, cute isn't it? I bought it when the three of us went to that store. It's called the angel series, and it's really popular with girls. They had pink and sky blue and green ones, too. Nanase bought a green notebook from the same series. We match."

I recognized it.

Miu had liked the series, too, and had sky blue notebooks and binders from it.

The past teased at my insides like black waves.

My throat tightened and it was getting harder to breathe; I struggled to drive the memory of Miu's face from my mind.

Somehow I forced out a few words without revealing my distress.

"Well, I'm glad you had fun. You've changed, Takeda. You're more exuberant than you used to be."

Takeda's mask seemed to slip away, and her face emptied as a smile pulled at her lips.

"I'm not having fun."

She looked at me with such a rational gaze that she seemed to be an entirely different person. The air suddenly grew cold.

"Not even a little bit. I'm only pretending to, because I don't want to destroy the mood."

Her voice was distant.

The girl standing before me was not the Chia Takeda who was so innocently puppylike, but another, lonelier Takeda who couldn't understand people's emotions.

I froze, speechless, and her childlike expression returned. She gave me an adorable smile.

"It doesn't take anything special to hide what you really think and put on an act. Everyone does it. And it's not so terrible being with you and Tohko."

I felt like there was something caught in my throat, but I forced out a smile, too.

"I see. I'm glad, then."

A smile that wasn't a lie, but a smile that wasn't true, either.

Takeda and I needed smiles like that. In order to avoid disrupting the climate between us. In order to maintain the outward appearance of peace.

"Let's go, Konoha!"

"Yeah."

I slung my bag over my shoulder and turned out the lights,

then left the darkened auditorium. We kept the same pace as we walked, Takeda talking gleefully about things that had happened in class or about her close friends.

I pretended not to know her secret and answered her with smiles.

Only my heart was as cold and heavy as lead.

But maybe everyone was like that.

Not just Takeda, but Akutagawa, Kotobuki, Tohko...Maybe they were all just pretending to be happy, but they weren't really inside. Maybe nobody spoke the truth and hid it away in order to maintain their precarious balance in society or at school.

Jerk — the sound of it echoed in my ear, and I felt an ache brush over my heart.

Smiling at everyone, being pleasant, not getting too close, not withdrawing too much, keeping just the right distance — I had been like that for a long time, because I couldn't bear to lose something important again. Because I hated the thought of hurting anyone or of being hurt.

Now, my days went by placidly. I didn't want to lose these peaceful, conventional hours that were nonetheless tepidly heartrending.

So Takeda and I were both likely to go on telling lies.

Outside, the sky was dyed scarlet. It looked like the end of the world.

As we passed by the side of the school building, Takeda suddenly tugged on my sleeve.

"Isn't that Akutagawa?"

Three slender shadows were cast on the wall behind the school.

The shadows danced about, washed in the deep red sunlight. One swung its arm up, and the other two drew together, seeming to tremble.

I saw Akutagawa and Sarashina...and a boy, a student I didn't recognize, all talking together very seriously.

Sarashina was shaking, on the verge of tears. Akutagawa stood as if to shield her, and the well-built boy glared at him murderously. He seemed to be yelling at Akutagawa fiercely. Akutagawa's brow was knit with distress as he watched the other boy. Every once in a while, his tightly shut lips would move slightly.

"It looks like it's gonna get violent," Takeda breathed, and at that same moment, the other boy threw a fist into Akutagawa's stomach.

Akutagawa doubled over and staggered on his feet.

Both of Sarashina's hands flew to her mouth, and she let out a frail scream.

Takeda and I both sucked in a breath, as well.

The boy threw a string of punches into Akutagawa's stomach and launched a kick at his chest. Though he staggered, Akutagawa held his ground and stayed on his feet. Sarashina tried to run forward, but he reached out a hand to stop her. He was punched again, but still he stood.

Should I get a teacher? But I was frozen, my legs turned to jelly. I couldn't tear my eyes from Akutagawa.

Sarashina clung to Akutagawa's back. He gently pushed her away, then slowly fell to his knees on the grass and bowed his head.

In the dark flames of the evening sun, he pressed his head to the ground and groveled. He looked like Christ being crucified when he did that.

A young man dressed in a black school uniform, rising out of the fading light. One who took suffering into his own body. A martyr.

My palms were sweating, and the inside of my mouth was dry.

My head throbbed with the knowledge that I had glimpsed something I shouldn't have.

The other boy's face twisted with frustration. He gave Akutagawa's shoulder a vicious kick, then yelled something at him and left.

Sarashina crumpled to her knees, buried her face in Akutagawa's back, and wept.

The sun set, and Akutagawa kept his forehead pressed against the ground, not moving, until faint, cool shadows hid them both.

We could only hold our breath and watch the scene play out like a painful fantasy.

Chapter 3 – I'll Slice It to Pieces

I received your letter.

As soon as I started reading it, I felt as if my heart was being torn open, and I grew dizzy.

You didn't grasp my reasons for distancing myself from you at all. The paper was wholly devoted to you calling me a coward and a liar, to you ordering me to carry out your one-sided desires, to curses on the past, to threats against me, and nothing else.

You're going to slit your wrists, you're going to jump out a window, you're going to drink poison — I want you to realize that writing these things down without giving it a second thought is foolishness that only diminishes your value.

I thought you had more pride than that.

I tried to understand that behind your apparent strength, you were possessed of a glasslike fragility, and that fragility hurts and consumes you. And that you are a prisoner of the past and pray for vengeance. I've watched your pain and suffering, your despair, your battles, and your tears all this time.

I wish with all my heart for your happiness. That's why I want you to know that dishonorable, malicious acts will tear your heart to shreds. Since your happiness will be my atonement, I mean to help you and will do so eagerly, as long as your desires are the right ones.

But I am not your slave.

I will not blanch at your threats and come running.

You are too dismissive of the man I am. You think I have no anger, no pain, no laments.

If I was to reveal what I desire most at this moment, you wouldn't be able to stop trembling. Of course, I'll refrain from writing it here.

My endurance is reaching its limit. I can't stand it any longer. I feel myself going crazy. Although I brought this on myself, matters beyond my control keep cropping up, and I keep passing sleepless nights.

Ever since the incident, I've believed I needed to be an honorable person. But now I've started to wonder who or what I have to be honorable for.

My father?

My mother?

My friends?

The past?

The future?

You?

⟹◈⟸

When I saw Akutagawa the next morning in class, he looked tired. I didn't immediately call out to him, but he looked up and smiled.

"Morning, Inoue."

His face was tranquil. My heart clenched as I awkwardly returned his greeting. "Morning, Akutagawa."

The day before, Takeda had said coolly, "We should leave it alone. I'm going to pretend like I didn't see anything."

That was probably the way to do it. You shouldn't stick your nose into other people's business, especially if you're not even friends. I should just treat him like I always did.

But each time I looked at Akutagawa's face, I was forced to remember what happened the day before. Even if we talked about it, I wouldn't be comfortable.

On the other hand, Kotobuki looked like she was still angry, and as soon as she saw me, she turned abruptly away and went over to Mori and the rest of her friends. That, too, was a vise on my heart.

Fifth period today was homeroom, and we made preparations for the comic book café we were doing for the culture fair. Everyone was making signs to hang out front or billboards of anime drawings to display inside or shelves to put the books in.

I was in the group making shelves and was cutting up cardboard with a box cutter.

Akutagawa painted billboards.

Several girls approached him, apparently to ask him to help with something. Akutagawa nodded and left his billboard, then went over to the standing signboard and pulled out a bent nail on the back support of the board before hammering in a new one.

"Thanks, Akutagawa."

The girls thanked him exuberantly. Akutagawa said something to them with a placid expression and went back to his billboard. The girls looked over at him and chattered enthusiastically.

"Man, Akutagawa's as popular as ever," I heard a boy working behind me say.

"But he doesn't want a girlfriend," said another.

"Wasn't there a rumor that he was dating a girl in his class in first year? You know, that pretty one. Sarashina."

The instant they mentioned Sarashina's name, my focus slipped and I lost my grip. It was right as I pulled the blade down on a piece of cardboard I was holding, and with the force behind the blade, I cut open the back of my left hand.

"Ow!"

"Ack, what're you doing, Inoue?!"

"Your hand's covered in blood!"

My classmates flocked around me in surprise. The blood flowing from the back of my hand fell onto the cardboard, staining it, and a girl screamed.

I was just about to tell them I was fine when someone pressed a gray handkerchief over the back of my hand. Then he took hold of my arm and pulled me up.

It was Akutagawa.

"I'll take him to the nurse," he told the class monitor, then whispered, "You okay?"

I nodded. "Y-yeah."

"Press down on it firmly."

He took my right hand and made me cover my left hand with it; then he put an arm around me and walked me out.

When we left the room, I saw Kotobuki standing perfectly still, her face ashen.

The nurse seemed to be out — there was no one in the office.

Akutagawa had me sit on a bed. He sat down in a chair, then cleaned my wound with a cotton pad soaked with disinfectant.

"Sorry...I can't believe I cut myself with a box cutter in high school."

After disinfecting the wound, he put some gauze on my hand

77

and wrapped it in medical tape. While he was securing it, he murmured, "Was there something on your mind?"

I couldn't tell him that I'd been thinking about him, so I said nothing. Akutagawa kept his face down and asked in a low voice, "You have something you want to ask me?"

I felt as if he had clamped his hand down on my heart.

His big, warm, strong hand kept a firm grasp on my left hand.

"You've looked like there was something you wanted to ask me all morning."

Had it been that obvious? My ears burned like the third-rate actor that I was.

I took a halting breath and tasted the bitter, medicinal air of the nurse's office. I opened my stubbornly unmoving mouth, and in a quiet voice I said, "Yesterday, I saw you getting beat up by a student I didn't recognize. And Sarashina was with you."

Akutagawa's hands paused as he laid the tape on my hand. A pained breath escaped his dry lips.

"Oh...you saw that."

"I'm sorry. I was going to pretend I hadn't seen anything. And actually, I knew about Sarashina before, too. She's...your girlfriend, right?"

I saw Akutagawa's face darken. He hung his head and a shadow passed over his eyes as the wrinkles between his eyebrows deepened, and I felt a chill.

"She's not my girlfriend."

"You said that before, too. But then why would she talk to me as if you two were still going out? Who was that beating you up yesterday? Why was he the only one throwing punches? You even had to grovel to him."

Once I'd opened my mouth, I couldn't stop. Akutagawa murmured in a rasping voice that seemed to stick in his throat, "It's... all my fault. It makes sense that he'd beat me up for what I did.

I'm a contemptible person…to Sarashina…and to Igarashi…
Of course they'd hate me."

I couldn't stand to see Akutagawa blame himself like this. It
was too painful.

As I struggled over whether I should stick my nose in or stay out
of it, I couldn't completely stop the awkward words that followed.

"Truly contemptible people don't call themselves that. Maybe
you just try too hard. You're upstanding and serious and honorable and considerate, but it must wear you out to be like that all
the time. Can't you just let go and relax every once in a while?"

Akutagawa lifted his eyes, and I started.

He glared at me, sparks flashing deep in his eyes. The usual
serenity on his face was gone; it was now tense and colored with a
violent rage.

"I'm not the upstanding guy you think I am!"

His voice was like a howl echoing through the room. He gripped
my freshly bandaged hand with such strength I was sure it would
shatter. A sharp pain stabbed through my brain. I almost screamed.

Akutagawa shouted, "You think I'm serious and honorable and
considerate?! You're wrong! I'm none of those things! You don't
know *anything*!"

Grinding my hand with his merciless strength, he brought his
face close to mine. His gaze with its naked displeasure; his pained,
explosive breathing; his trembling blue lips all told of his murder-
ous rage and insanity. My entire body prickled with cold goose
bumps, and terror bolted down my spine.

"For a long time, I've messed up other people's lives. Like
Omiya, I put on a front and act honorable, but I'm still an awful,
contemptible person, and I betray the people who trust me!"

I was afraid; my hand hurt so much. I couldn't budge, a hos-
tage to his raging emotions. The things he said cascaded into my
heart like a black torrent.

"I can't ever let down my guard—I have to keep strict control over myself forever. But I can't fight back the impulses. I bet you have no idea what I'm thinking right now. Do you, Inoue? How I feel? What I wish I could actually do? The terrible things I think about? You don't know! What a tainted person I am…Inoue, you—you couldn't even begin to understand it!"

Gritting his teeth fiercely, he glared at me, violence glinting in his eyes.

Who was this person?

He wasn't the Akutagawa I knew.

All of a sudden, Akutagawa released his grip on my hand and his face grew pained and morose.

"…I'm going to hurt you, Inoue," he said in a rough voice, then stood up. "You should forget this ever happened. Don't get close to me.

"Sorry," he murmured painfully, then left the nurse's office.

Left by myself, I hugged my arms around myself and shuddered as a frigid feeling climbed up my legs.

Only the wound on my left hand—which he had gripped so hard—burned like fire. A red stain spread slowly through the gauze.

"You don't know…Inoue…You couldn't even begin to understand it."

The words he had hurled at me stabbed my heart. As my throat tightened and a searing pain burned my skin, the memories sealed in the depths of my mind returned to vivid life.

Her lighthearted voice calling me, *Konoha—Konoha.* Her sweet eyes peeking up at me teasingly. Her bobbing ponytail.

"Konoha, I don't think you would ever understand."

Miu murmured, turning around in front of the railing on the roof and smiling sadly; then she tumbled backward.

I remembered the scene vividly. Miu's face overshadowed Akutagawa's, and I sat staring into space.

The stabbing chill wouldn't stop, and the core of my mind ached with implacable terror.

No —

Leave him alone.

If you get any closer to Akutagawa —

———————◇———————

Several times a day, a beastlike anger wells up from the depths of my heart.

When I ask myself if I would ever hurt someone just because I felt like it, my vision clouds over and I break into a cold sweat.

How can I quiet this infernal impulse?

Don't come after me. I have no idea what I might do.

The sensation I felt when I cut up the library books comes again and again to my mind.

The desk so far off, no one speaking, hearing only the sound of my own breathing and the pages turning in the tense silence. The loneliness and the terror that maybe I was the only person alive in this corner of the world. The self-loathing I felt about what I was planning to do.

In the midst of all that, I took the box cutter out of my bag, pressed it down on the center fold of the page, and drew it smoothly down. When it was completely free of the book, my spirit felt strangely liberated and unburdened.

My head aches, and I yearn for that feeling of floating in the air.

I want to cut something up.

A book — no, something softer, warmer, purer...

Maybe then I'll be free of this suffering that seems to burn my heart.

Maybe then I wouldn't hear that voice blaming me every night. I can't go see you like this. Please understand. I'm standing on the very precipice.

⇒◆⇐

Before sixth period started, I went back to my class. I offered my concerned classmates noncommittal answers and sat down.

Akutagawa flipped through a notebook at his own desk. I looked over at him, jumped, then hurriedly looked away and began arranging my books on my desk. It was stifling even to be in the same room with him.

While I was mopping the floor in the hallway during cleanup, Kotobuki came over and reached out her hand at me with a frown. "Let me have that."

"Wha—?"

"You're barely pushing at all. What's the point?"

She grabbed the mop from me while I stood still, perplexed, and she began efficiently scrubbing the floor.

"You must really be stupid to cut your hand with a box cutter. What an idiot."

"Uh...well, thanks."

"I just want to be done with cleanup."

Kotobuki pursed her lips as she spoke, then turned her back on me.

"Inoue, did you have a fight with Akutagawa?"

"Why do you ask?"

"Akutagawa came back alone, and I don't think you guys talked at all afterward."

"...You're just imagining things," I murmured feebly, which made Kotobuki turn back around and glare at me angrily.

"Well, it's none of my business."

Now that she mentioned it, Akutagawa didn't seem to be in the classroom. Had he gone somewhere? No — better not to inquire. I couldn't get involved with Akutagawa anymore.

"You're gonna make it to rehearsals today, right?"

"S-sure," I answered, stumbling over my words. In the nurse's office, Akutagawa had asked me to forget about what I'd seen, but would I be able to act like everything was normal? I was so terrified of facing him that I trembled.

I went back into the classroom with Kotobuki once she finished mopping.

Kotobuki glanced at the bag hanging on the side of her desk, and her eyes widened.

"That's weird."

She was scrutinizing a string looped on her bag.

"What's wrong?"

"My rabbit is missing."

"What?"

"The one I bought when we all went to that store with Tohko. Oh no. Did I lose it somewhere?"

Her gaze fell to the floor; shock and tears were in her eyes.

"Want me to help you look for it?"

"That's okay. You go on ahead."

"But —"

"It's fine."

She said it so forcefully that all I could do was leave the room without her.

Feeling as if I was hugging a heavy rock to my chest, I started walking toward the music hall. My eyes turned toward the back of the school building, as if drawn there, and there I saw Akutagawa, his back turned. I felt like I'd been hit by lightning.

Standing straight and tall, Akutagawa turned to face me.

He held something fluffy and white in his right hand.

It was a rabbit.

Not a doll but what looked like the real thing.

Red blood dripped from the soft white fur that covered its throat. Akutagawa's hand was also stained red where he held the rabbit by its ears.

Overcome by a violent nausea, I bolted.

Why did he have that rabbit? What had he done? These questions tumbled through my mind, and at the same time a terror chilled my entire body and crept into my heart. All I could think was that I had to get away from him immediately.

Akutagawa was terrifying.

Terrifying!

I didn't go to the music hall. I ran through the school gates and went straight home.

I went into my room and closed the door, sat down, and rested my elbows on my desk; then cradled my head.

The throbbing of my heart was out of control. The steely glare Akutagawa had given me in the nurse's office alternated with the gaze hardened by loathing that Miu had once turned on me, and I screamed out, "Stop!"

Why?! We had had a comfortable relationship where all we did was talk pleasantly and compare our answers to homework.

Why did you show me the violence of your emotions? Why did you turn your hatred on me?

Miu — Miu had done the same.

Like Nojima who was so in love with Sugiko, I had been smitten with Miu. I'd believed that Miu liked me, too. We were the best of friends and passed our every day in laughter. But then that day in our third year of middle school, Miu had fallen off the roof of the school right in front of me.

"Konoha, I don't think you would ever understand."

Leaving behind those mysterious words.

That summer, my world was destroyed.

Even now, I didn't understand why Miu did it. Was it my fault she jumped? Had I done something to her?

I felt like delicate white fingers were crushing my heart, and I clenched the front of my shirt in my fist. My throat was dry, my vision wavered like a mirage, and my breathing grew erratic. I staggered and collapsed into bed, taking short, panting breaths, and desperately tried to calm my body as it offered up a scream.

When I came to my senses, I closed my eyes. My shoulders heaved with my breathing. The sweat pouring from me soaked my shirt and hair uncomfortably.

I still hadn't forgotten about Miu.

I was sick of this. It was unbearable to have intertwined your heart so deeply with another, to believe in your future, and then to suddenly be denied it.

My time with Miu would have been plentiful.

In the corner of one half-opened eye, I spotted my copy of *Friendship*, which had been tossed on the floor. I must have knocked it to the floor when I'd gotten up from my desk before.

Sweat dripped into my eyes as I gazed bitterly at the blurry book, thinking.

Akutagawa had attacked me, his gaze clouded and filled with dark despair. He must be holding a secret he couldn't tell anyone and be suffering just like Omiya.

But it was best that I didn't find out what that was. We weren't even friends. I couldn't worry about why Akutagawa had been so enraged by what I'd said in the nurse's office or what was up with that rabbit or any of it!

Tonight's dinner seemed to lodge behind my ribs, and I wound up leaving half of it.

"I guess...I'm not feeling so good. It's fine. I'm sure it'll be better tomorrow," I said, making up an excuse for my concerned mother.

When my tiny sister begged to play a game, I apologized and said, "Sorry, Maika. Not today. I'll play with you tomorrow." I patted her on the head and retreated to my room.

I turned off the lights and lay in my bed, staring into the dark, listening to a soothing ballad on my headphones when my door opened and my mother came in.

"Konoha, are you asleep? You have a phone call from Amano."

I took off my headphones and got up.

"Thanks. I'll take it."

Once my mother had disappeared behind the door, I picked up the phone.

"Hello..."

A voice so feeble it made even me sad slipped past my lips.

Tohko had probably called because I skipped out on rehearsal and went straight home.

Just as I'd expected, I heard her bright voice on the other end.

"Konoha!! You can't skip club activities without so much as telling your president. Nanase was worried."

"Sorry. After I left class, I suddenly started feeling awful."

"Really?" she inquired serenely. There was a soft, kind aspect to her voice, much like the music I'd been listening to. "A president can tell when you're lying. I bet you didn't want to run into Akutagawa, did you?"

Surprised, I asked, "Did he talk to you?"

Tohko chortled.

"So that *is* it. Akutagawa was late to rehearsals today, too. When he heard you weren't there yet, he looked pained and only said, 'Oh, I see.' He seemed to know why you wouldn't come. So I imagined that something might have happened between you two."

"You're awful. You tricked me."

"Never underestimate a book girl," she said pompously, robbing me of all my energy.

Geez, why did she always get the better of me? It sucked. It made no sense.

"Heh-heh. Now grit your teeth, and tell your president *everything*."

Urged on by her musical voice, I started telling her in a whisper about what was going on with Akutagawa.

Tohko heard me out, occasionally encouraging me to continue in gentle, breathy tones. Once I'd finished my tale, she meekly said, "You know, I heard at the library that some books were cut up again. A Jane Yolen collection, a Hakushū Kitahara collection of poetry, plus a collection of children's stories by Ju Mukuhato and short stories by Sakyo Komatsu... And this happened a little while ago, but one of the kids in the biology club told me that one of the rabbits they were taking care of disappeared and they've been looking for it."

A chill went through my hand as I held the phone.

Library books were being cut up again? And then a rabbit disappeared?

"But I don't think Akutagawa is the one who cut up the books. This time or the time before," Tohko said suddenly in an excited voice, leaving me agape. "Hey, do you want to help me find out *the truth*, Konoha?"

———※———

What foolish things I continue to do, Mother.

I can't pretend that my recent letter to you was rational. But if I stop writing letters, I doubt I'll be able to contain the crazed impulses inside me.

I yelled at Inoue today. I know that he doesn't mean any harm and that he's worried about me. But his fragility and sensitivity incensed me, and all of a sudden I wanted to hurt him.

Inoue didn't come to rehearsal after school. I had no idea how I was going to face him, so honestly I was relieved.

On the other hand, her psychological state has grown much more precarious, and I have no way of controlling her any longer. I buried the dead rabbit, whose throat had been slit, under a cherry tree at the back of the school yard. No matter how much I washed, the blood marks wouldn't go away. It made me sick.

You must be worried about me after my recent letters, Mother. I'm sure they don't make any sense to you. But I can't reveal this to anyone but you.

When you gave birth to me, you pushed yourself too hard and your health deteriorated.

So I've tried my best to be an upstanding person and not be a burden on you. To not make you worry, to not make our relatives pity you for having me, to never make you feel sad.

But that day six years ago, I destroyed others' lives through my dishonorable actions, and as punishment, I lost you.

And despite that, I've done another dishonorable thing.

Oh Mother, Mother, how foolish will your son become?

<hr />

At lunch the next day, I took a boxed lunch my mother had made for me to the book club room. Tohko had gotten there first and sat with her legs pulled up on a fold-up chair, eating her "food."

A copy of Françoise Sagan's *Do You Like Brahms?* rested on her knees. She would turn a page, then delicately tear it out and make a hushed chewing sound and swallow, then smile ecstatically.

"Sagan has the refined taste of a city. It's a beautiful, brisk, elegant flavor like a duck terrine in the hors d'oeuvres of French cuisine.

"Her subtle psychological description of a woman wavering between her flirtatious older lover and the gorgeous young man several years her junior, who loves her passionately, is truly amazing!

"It's like you're enjoying the rustic flavor of duck and the subtle texture of the terrine, and then the amber-colored consommé gelée paired with it makes your mouth quiver at the complexity of the sensation, which makes your heart squeeze tight. When Sagan was eighteen years old, she debuted with *Hello Sadness*, the story of a true-to-life seventeen-year-old girl. But when she wrote this story about a middle-aged woman of thirty-nine as its heroine, she was only twenty-four."

As she expounded on the book, I stayed bent over the lunch my mother had made for me, eating.

"What did you mean when...you said that yesterday?" I asked in a murmur, and Tohko's voice turned cheerful again.

"You mean when I said we should find out 'the truth'?"

"Not that," I responded, raising my head.

Tohko had been smiling indulgently, so heat shot through my ears. I looked back down and muttered, "When you said Akutagawa wasn't the one cutting up library books. You *saw* him cutting a page out with his box cutter."

I hadn't been able to talk to him much in class today, either. He'd asked me how my hand was, and it had taken everything I had to say that it was fine. He seemed to find it difficult, too. I didn't want to interact with him again; I knew that with all of my heart. So then why had I gone along with Tohko's suggestion and come here?

Tohko closed the book she'd been eating.

"Sure, we witnessed Akutagawa cutting pages out of that Takeo Arishima book. But look, Konoha."

She picked the book up, held it out to me, and flipped through the pages.

The book was almost split in two by all the places where the pages had been cut out. As she continued flipping through the pages, others fell out. And two or three times after that...

"See? It's not just cut in one place. All Akutagawa cut out was one page, remember? And look at this."

Tohko slid her finger down the length of the page below the one that had been cut out. There was a single line about a tenth of an inch from the book's center.

"All of the lines are away from the center fold. The mark from the knife is left on the page underneath. So don't you think it's strange that there's a mark here, too?" she asked gently, pointing out the two equidistant lines.

"Maybe this was cut with something other than a box cutter. I'm sure this book had pages missing before Akutagawa started cutting. But when we talked to him here in the club room, he didn't say a word about it. He was talking as if it was the first time he'd ever cut a book. So I thought maybe there was someone else cutting up books. Maybe it was that person cutting up the other books, not Akutagawa."

"Akutagawa might have cut them all. You have no proof, after all."

"That's true. But Akutagawa's not the sort of person who would do something like that without a reason."

"That's just what you think. Couldn't the real Akutagawa be different from the one we know?"

I remembered the expression twisted by hatred that he'd given me in the nurse's office, and the core of my body trembled with cold.

"It's still a fact that Akutagawa cut that book up right in front of us, though. If he's not the culprit, then why would he go to the trouble of doing that? His explanation is still more convincing. He was cutting books up out of stress."

Tohko murmured gloomily, "He could be covering for someone."

Then she looked at me a little sadly.

"You know, I asked one of the archery team members in my class about Akutagawa. He said when Akutagawa was in first year, one of the second-years harassed him. He made Akutagawa clean up by himself and forced him to follow an impossible practice regimen that strained his body. He also made him run dozens of laps around the school without any shoes on. My classmate said he felt bad for Akutagawa."

"Who was this second-year?"

"Igarashi, the guy you saw behind the school. He's in third year now."

The image of the muscular boy in the school uniform, his shoulders broader than Akutagawa's, resurfaced in my mind. He'd beaten Akutagawa up behind the school without suffering any blows in return, and Akutagawa had even groveled to him.

"Apparently at first, Igarashi was a good mentor to Akutagawa. He had a high opinion of Akutagawa and chatted with him a lot. He was very fond of him. And apparently, Akutagawa had a lot of respect for Igarashi, too."

"Why did Igarashi start tormenting him?"

Sarashina's face flashed through a corner of my mind. Behind the school, she had clung to Akutagawa's back and wept. I knew she was involved somehow.

Tohko's response was exactly what I'd imagined.

"My classmate told me that Akutagawa stole the girl that Igarashi had been dating. A second-year named Sarashina. She was in Akutagawa's class last year."

A sigh escaped me.

So Sarashina was the cause of it, after all.

Thinking back on the situation now, Akutagawa had seemed to hate Omiya, who had betrayed his best friend by choosing Sugiko. When I had tried to compliment him and said that he was perfect for the role, he'd looked bitter, and when Tohko and the other girls had been in a tizzy over whether Omiya or Nojima was cooler, he'd had some harsh criticism for Omiya.

He must have had Igarashi and Sarashina in mind. He had identified with Omiya, and it had pained him.

"Akutagawa was the one who first introduced Igarashi to Sarashina, it seems. At first, the three of them would go out together. That was last summer. Then around the end of autumn, Igarashi's attitude toward Akutagawa changed. His bullying got real bad, and when a third-year couldn't stand to watch it anymore, he asked what was going on. Igarashi apparently told him that Akutagawa had stolen his girlfriend. And Akutagawa didn't deny it. He said, 'Igarashi is right. It's all my fault.' After that, Igarashi quit the archery team."

Tohko drooped.

What she'd told me was nothing more than a run-of-the-mill love triangle. Falling for an upperclassman's girl happened all the time and so did hooking up with your friend's girlfriend on the sly. It was everywhere in books and on TV.

There were even love triangles at the turn of the century, and even before that — ever since the age of legend, people had reenacted moronic love stories of stealing and being stolen from, of falling in love and breaking up.

But for those involved, it probably wasn't so easy to accept.

Omiya agonized over the knowledge of his crime against Nojima, and like him, Akutagawa must have blamed himself fiercely. In the nurse's office, he'd told me that everything was his fault.

"I'm a contemptible person... Of course they'd hate me."

Wait — but why would Sarashina hate him? I could understand Igarashi since his girlfriend had been taken from him. But why Sarashina? When she was clinging to Akutagawa, it definitely didn't look like she hated him.

It was strange. There had to be something more going on between Akutagawa and Sarashina...

Just as I seized on this question, a paralyzing anxiety welled up in me. I couldn't. Hadn't I decided I wouldn't get involved?

My breathing grew labored, and in a quiet voice, I said, "Tohko... you said before that maybe Akutagawa was covering for someone? Considering what you just said, the only people important enough to Akutagawa — or the only ones he owed enough — to protect would be Sarashina and Igarashi."

"Yeah."

Tohko nodded.

"Which one do you think he's protecting, Tohko?"

"I —"

As she hesitantly opened her blushing pink lips, a beeping sound started in Tohko's pocket. She pulled out not a cell phone, but her beloved silver stopwatch. Apparently it had a regular clock in it, too, because she looked at it and then her eyes went wide.

"Omigosh. Lunch is over in five minutes!"

We both bolted to our feet and rushed out of the room. As we ran down the hall, Tohko explained quickly, "I'm not quite sure yet who's cutting up books. Or why they did it."

Tohko pulled to a stop in front of the stairwell where we would part ways.

"I thought it might scare you so I wasn't going to say anything, but I heard another rabbit has disappeared from the biology club. A girl from the club was worrying about it this morning."

I recalled the rabbit, held by its ears, blood dripping from it, and I gulped. Tohko grabbed my arm and pulled me closer to murmur encouragingly into my ear, "Look, you absolutely cannot miss rehearsal today. We're doing the costumes today. Not for any reason, okay? Promise?"

Her warm breath struck my ear, and her soft lips brushed it for an instant, then pulled away.

"See you after school! If you skip, I'm going to your house to get you!"

She smiled, then ran up the stairs.

Tohko... I can see up your skirt. Are those shorts?... But no.

They were white.

My ears and cheeks slowly grew warmer. I hurried off to my own classroom.

And just then, Akutagawa cut across my vision as he walked down the hall.

I felt as if someone had thrown water into my burning face.

Fifth period was about to start. Where could he be going? Was Akutagawa *cutting class*?

Oops, no—I'll pretend I didn't see him. Don't even think about following him. You can't get involved!

I was so violently torn that I felt my throat dry out, but my feet betrayed me and moved in the direction Akutagawa had disappeared.

When I turned a corner in the hallway, I heard the sound of footsteps descending the stairs. Holding my breath and listening carefully, I followed him. Overhead, the bell rang announcing the start of fifth period. I was jumpy, wanting to get back to class, but I couldn't keep my feet from following him. Cold sweat spread over the back of my neck.

We arrived at the open area where all the shoe lockers were. Hiding behind an aluminum locker, I searched for Akutagawa.

Then I spotted him standing in front of our class's lockers.

He looked down harshly at an envelope he held in his hands. Had he taken it out of his locker just now?

It was not the white rectangular envelopes I'd seen before, but rather a sky blue envelope with white angel wings on it. It was from the same collection as Takeda's binder, the one Miu had liked. A girl must have given it to him.

I sensed a fierce rage in Akutagawa's expression, and I shrank back.

When I'd seen Akutagawa standing at the mailboxes before, he had always worn a morose, pained expression.

But now his eyes were filled with a fiery hostility and anger.

Akutagawa tore the letter.

My heart jumped at the sound.

He tore the letter a second time, walked over to the trash can beside the lockers, and started to throw the note away.

But then he stopped.

He groaned quietly and narrowed his eyes, looking troubled. He gritted his teeth firmly, closed his hand around the rumpled letter, and shoved it roughly into his pants pocket.

That was all I saw. I ran back to class, unable to hold back the tension that was crushing my chest.

The teacher wasn't there yet.

About ten minutes later in the middle of class, Akutagawa opened the door at the back of the room.

"I'm sorry. I was looking for something in the library."

He bowed to the teacher and sat down. My eyes had already shot to his pants pocket, but as far as I could tell from the outside, there was nothing unusual about it.

Who had that letter been from...?

That question tangled gloomily in my heart, along with the thought that I couldn't get involved.

⟸⬦⟹

Do you like me, I wonder?

You said so in a letter you sent me without the slightest hesitation.

Ever since the incident, I've avoided becoming close to the opposite sex, and I thought for sure I would never be in love.

But that winter, when I saw you — you glared at me as if you were looking at the filthiest, most loathsome creature in the world, and when you attacked me, I felt hot stabs of pain in my heart.

I thought you were beautiful, though you abused me mercilessly. I was captivated by the vivid blush of your cheek, the sharpness in your glinting eye, and I couldn't look away.

I knew only too well that you had not a shred of desire to accept me. That you wanted only to satisfy your own dark, cruel cravings.

And I was not the sort of illustrious person who might win your heart.

But I couldn't stop myself from going to you. I wanted to see you and receive your cold gaze. I wanted to hear your voice hurl abuse at me.

Perhaps I wanted you to blame me.

Everyone heaped praise on me for being an honorable and upstanding person. So maybe I wanted to be reminded that it wasn't true—that I was a despicable person who deserved your abuse.

You wanted to ask me about school.

How did I spend my day? Did I have any friends? Did I have a girlfriend?

You asked, claws hidden in each word, and listened to what I told you with a pale, tense face. Then in the end, you would always get upset and say, "Go away."

So gradually I started to say ugly things about what I'd done in the past, until one day you pressed me for a decision.

I know what it was that set you off. I also know that you were still fighting memories of the past, trapped by them, slashed by them, while you writhed in pain in an unescapable, pitch-black labyrinth.

I want to grant your wish.

Because it will be my atonement.

But even if I can save you, I'd still be a contemptible traitor if I did that.

Your wish is dirty! It's not right! It hurts people!

And yet you want me to do it? You order me to do something that's not honorable?

Please stop sending me letters. Stop writing things that test my spirit.

I know I'll be taken in by you. I recognize that. But I can't be any more foolish than I already am.

⟫◆⟪

"Wow, you two are *adorable!*"

Kotobuki and Takeda had changed into kimonos with long, trailing sleeves tucked into empire-waisted and full-pleated pants, and when she saw them, Tohko gave a shout of joy.

Kotobuki had clipped extensions on either side of her head and tied red ribbons in them. She fidgeted in embarrassment.

When classes ended, I'd been conflicted over whether or not I should go home when Kotobuki planted herself in front of me, her arms crossed over her chest. "We're doing costume fitting today. You can't skip." Then she pursed her lips and glared at me.

"Hey Akutagawa! Don't drag your feet, either! We're going to rehearsal."

Somehow she managed to settle things and chased me and Akutagawa into the auditorium.

Dressed up as Sugiko, she was like a different person. Her cheeks were delicately flushed, and she kept her eyes down. Apparently they had asked a third-year who did tea ceremony for the clothes. I was busy being impressed by how clothes could change a girl when Kotobuki glanced over and stuck her lip out.

"Wh-what are you looking at? You got a problem?"

"No, I was just thinking how good you look in old-style clothes," I told her honestly, but she turned bright red.

"You—you jerk! Why would you say that?! You're just giving me more empty flattery! I—I can't believe what a jerk you are!"

"But...it's the truth."

"What?!"

Kotobuki was speechless. I smiled. "You and Takeda look really good."

"Yaaay! Thank you, Konoha!"

Takeda wore a trailing, navy ribbon in her hair. She swung her long sleeves and giggled.

In contrast, Kotobuki grumbled discontentedly. "I *really* hate you, Inoue!" And she turned away pointedly.

Huh? Wh-why was she mad at me?

I was confused. But Tohko came bouncing over to me, elated.

"Oooh, I was so conflicted about whether we should do elegant

young ladies in fluttering kimonos or go with the pants, too, but this is a total blowout! A 1920s romance simply demands ribbons and billowing, high-waisted pants!"

Tohko was wearing a Western-style shirt with a stiff collar and a resist-dyed kimono over it. Akutagawa and I were dressed similarly.

"Heh-heh. You look totally different, too, Tohko! It looks great!"

"Ohh, you mean it?"

"Yup! I feel faint!"

"Oh, stop! Maybe girls will send me bunches of love letters."

Tohko's eyes glazed over dreamily, probably imagining the love advice mailbox in the school yard stuffed full of sugary, handwritten love letters. The shirt and kimono over her chest lay perfectly flat, and that didn't look strange in the slightest, just as I had expected, but her long braids swinging like cats' tails made her look nothing like a Japanese boy. Just as this thought crossed my mind, she pulled on a dark brown tweed cap and stuffed her long braids into it.

"Now I look even more like a beautiful young man, no?"

"Yes! It makes me want to sigh your name all dreamily!" said Takeda.

"Do it, do it!"

"Ohhh, *Toh*ko!"

"Oh, Chia!"

The two were completely into it. They fell into each other's arms and shrieked and everything.

"You're getting a little carried away, Takeda."

Kotobuki looked sullen, but then Takeda threw her arms around her.

"Ohhh, I love you, too, Nanase! My big sister!"

"Hey — quit it! Let go of me!"

Nanase's eyes darted around in panic as Takeda embraced her.

I tried to keep a low profile in the midst of that animated scene and furtively watched Akutagawa.

He seemed to be thinking about something, a bleak expression on his face. The dark colors of the clothes suited his ramrod straight height, and he gave off a straitlaced charm and sexy self-denial. I was sure the female audience members would be transfixed. But shadows darkened his downcast eyes.

I felt a twinge in my heart. I was afraid if I watched him too long, I would be drawn in by the pain he faced, so I quickly looked away.

"All right, let's start practicing," Tohko called out, beginning the dress rehearsal.

We started with the Ping-Pong competition between Sugiko and Omiya, where Sugiko defeats her older brother's friends one after another with her astute Ping-Pong skills and everyone cheers for her.

"Why not have Nojima try next?"

Nojima was nonplussed by the suggestion from Hayakawa, who was a rival for Sugiko's love. He wasn't good at Ping-Pong. But everyone goaded him on, and he was on the brink of being forced into facing off against Sugiko when Omiya stepped forward.

"Why don't I stand in for him?"

Just then, the chest of Akutagawa's kimono vibrated.

Akutagawa's face tensed. My breath caught, too.

"Sorry," he murmured angrily, then took his phone out to check the screen.

The very next moment, his eyes seemed to pop out of his head and he gulped.

"I'll be right back. Sorry, really," he offered hurriedly; then he bit down on his lip and left the stage.

"Oh — Akutagawa!" Tohko called to him, but he didn't turn around. He ran up between the seats and left the auditorium.

We all looked at each other uneasily.

"He did that before, too. Looked at his phone and then ran out."

"I wonder what happened."

Takeda's gaze landed subtly on me. I recalled Akutagawa groveling behind the school. Igarashi had been hitting him, and Akutagawa had offered no resistance.

If Igarashi was the one calling him...

Whatever. It was none of my business. There was nothing I could do anyway. Don't think about it anymore.

Just then, something fluttered across the stage.

By the time I realized it was the long sleeve of Tohko's kimono, she was already running frenetically down from the stage. Her cap flew off and her supple braids danced behind her.

"Konoha, let's go!"

"*Where* exactly?"

I gaped. Lifting the hem of her kimono and cinching it up between her thighs, she answered, "After Akutagawa!"

With her legs now exposed, Tohko ran up the aisle between the seats.

I hurried off the stage and chased after her. When they saw that, even Kotobuki and Takeda followed in their trailing sleeves and billowing pants.

Tramping down the hallway outside the small auditorium, passing through the atrium, bursting out of the building, and then running off again, Tohko was far from the beauty in men's clothing or the modest book girl. She was more like the fishwife carrying a scale over her shoulders in a samurai drama or a female firefighter running to the site of a conflagration.

As I ran, I wondered how I'd managed to jump straight into the fire even though I had meant to stay out of Akutagawa's business from now on. I also thought about how I really ought to just go back.

But since Tohko was running on right ahead of me, her braids streaming behind her, I could hardly go back by myself. Who knew *what* Tohko would do if I took my eyes off her!

The students we passed looked at us in shock.

"Wait! Tohko, wait!"

Tohko was sprinting and apparently didn't hear me. Not that it mattered, but did Tohko know where Akutagawa had gone? She was running pretty hard.

But it looked like Tohko had made another one of her guesses, and once outside the school building, she plowed through to the back. She probably wanted to peek behind it into the back of the school yard.

Just then, we heard an earsplitting scream.

"Noooooo!"

That was a girl's voice! It sounded like Sarashina!

The moment we rounded the corner of the building, Tohko stopped and stood rooted to the spot. Once again, my heart was pierced by a scene out of a nightmare, happening right before my eyes.

Behind me, Kotobuki let out a squeak as she gulped back a scream.

Akutagawa stood with a chisel in his hand. Blood dripped from the V-shaped blade. A muscular boy had fallen to his knees in front of him. A pool of blood was spreading over the ground, and Akutagawa looked down at it blankly.

Sarashina was beside Akutagawa, kneeling on the grass, the front of her uniform splattered in blood. She was holding her head and sobbing.

"*No!* Why! Why did you do that?! It's that girl's fault! She did this! That girl *stabbed* him!" said Sarashina.

Suddenly someone grabbed my arm.

It was Kotobuki.

She was trembling, her eyes wide. She staggered and almost fell, but I supported her.

Takeda watched the scene, her face calm. Tohko stood perfectly still, her back to me.

People started to gather, drawn by Sarashina's cries. Several girls behind us screamed. Teachers elbowed their way through the crowd.

They fell speechless and gasped at the carnage before them. Akutagawa stood up straighter, and in a brittle voice devoid of emotion, he said, "I stabbed Igarashi."

⟹◆⟸

I've reached my limit. I can't sleep. Even when I lie down in bed, despite being so tired my body feels like it's made of clay, my mind is ringing and alert, and a ferocious creature rampages through my heart.

There was another letter from you today. How much time you must have spent in writing it. Was that also because of your hatred? Do you hate me that much? Can't you forgive me? Please, don't blame me. I'm a weak human being. I can't stand to be blamed anymore.

At home, I've tried sticking my box cutter into the tatami floor, into the sliding doors, into my notebooks, into my textbooks, into the rabbit. I cut my English book to shreds and scattered the pages around my head like confetti; I carved crosses into the sliding doors; I cut off the rabbit's feet.

But the mist doesn't clear. The bellowing in my heart never

stops. And the girl with the chisel stabbed into her chest continues to blame me.

I want to cut them out, cut them apart, break them into pieces, all of it, everything, you, the world, the past, the future, truth, lies; I want to cut them apart, cut them apart, cut them apart, cut them apart —

Mother, I've gone crazy.

Chapter 4 – Girl from the Past

Akutagawa's house was a Japanese-style building in a quiet residential neighborhood thirty minutes away from school by bus and then another ten-minute walk.

The day after the incident, Tohko and I went over to his house.

The chisel had sliced Igarashi in the chest and throat, and after being treated at the hospital, he was convalescing at home. His wounds hadn't been serious considering how much blood he'd lost, but he wasn't saying a word about what happened.

Sarashina had evidently taken quite a shock, and she had stayed home from school as well. Akutagawa had been ordered to stay at home for a while by the head teacher.

Everyone in class had found out about the incident, and the class was already abuzz about it first thing in the morning.

Takeda and Tohko came to my class to see how things were going, wearing gloomy expressions. So did Kotobuki, who had leaned against me trembling yesterday.

"So Akutagawa didn't come today?"

"I still can't believe he would stab someone."

"They're saying that…Igarashi called him out to talk about Sarashina, and they fought, and then Akutagawa stabbed him."

"Yeah. But what was Akutagawa doing with a chisel?"

"That's a good question! That's weird. I don't think he took anything with him when he ran out of the auditorium."

"…I wonder what he's doing right now."

"And what are we going to do about the play?"

Kotobuki and Takeda drooped. Trying to cheer them up, Tohko said, "After school, Konoha and I will go to his house."

I couldn't mount a protest against that.

I stood next to Tohko at the gate, which was adorned with an inked sign reading AKUTAGAWA, and looked up at the house.

"His house is magnificent."

"…Sure is."

To be honest, I was overcome by a desire to turn right around and go home.

Even if we saw Akutagawa, I had no idea what we would talk about or what we should tell him. My whole stomach was knotting up.

I didn't want to do this…I didn't want to go any farther.

But Tohko went briskly through the gate, and walking across the rocks that were sunk into the ground, she went to the front door and pressed the intercom.

"Yes, who is it?"

A young woman's voice answered. Tohko told the girl that she'd come to see Akutagawa and the door opened, a pretty girl's face appearing behind it. She had dyed brown, shoulder-length hair and wore jeans. She looked around twenty years old.

I moved up beside Tohko to greet her, and she introduced herself. "I'm Kazushi's oldest sister, Ayame." Then she smiled awkwardly. "Thank you for thinking of him." His family must have been upset by what happened.

"Wait here, I'll go get Kazushi."

She went up the massive wooden stairs.

"Kazushi, you have visitors. Can you hear me?"

There was the sound of a door sliding open, and Ayame's cries pierced my ears.

"What are you doing, Kazushi?!"

Tohko pulled her shoes off and went inside, then ran up the stairs. I went swiftly after her.

Ayame stood frozen in front of the open door to a room, her face colorless.

The twelve-foot-square, traditional-style room was in a horrifying state.

The many awards hanging on the walls, the sliding door, the shutters — all were cut up, lengthwise and at angles. Books, notes, and schoolbooks were tossed all over the floor, the marks of wild cuts from a blade left on their covers and pages.

Then there were what must have been homemade cookies or cupcakes scattered everywhere with their crumpled-up wrappers and cute red or pink ribbons beside them. The surfaces of the cakes were spotted with a purple mold that looked like blood pooled in a corpse.

I felt sick and clamped down on my throat.

In the center of the room, Akutagawa sat dressed in a shirt and slacks.

His eyes were devoid of spirit like those of a dead fish, his half-open lips were dry, and he had a tight hold on a folded-up box cutter in his right hand. Blood was dripping from its tip.

The sleeve was rolled up on his left arm, exposing several cuts with fresh red blood flowing from them. A pink rabbit doll lay unceremoniously beside him as he sat in a daze, its head and limbs cut off, soaking up the blood that dripped onto it.

"Kazushi, what — what have you done?! Your arm is bleeding." Ayame's voice was shaking.

Akutagawa murmured, his eyes still dry, "I cut myself…just to see. It's so easy to cut through…human skin."

Ayame's face tensed in horror.

"W-we have to bandage it."

She reached out to him hesitantly, but Akutagawa swatted her away. His listless face twisted ominously, and a cracked voice broke from his blue lips.

"No! This is my atonement! *Kanomata still hasn't forgiven me! Kanomata's wounds still haven't healed!*"

A jolt went through Ayame, and she froze. Tohko moved past her and took hold of Akutagawa's hand — the one that held the box cutter.

It was so sudden, I couldn't stop her. Akutagawa looked up at her in confusion.

"What are you doing here?"

"Because you're making your friends worry."

His grip slackened in surprise, and she took the blade from him.

"Hold onto that, Konoha."

She stretched an arm out to give it to me, and I hastily accepted it.

"Ayame, bring a bowl of water and some towels! And Konoha, you call a taxi!"

<hr/>

Why did the two of us meet?

When I was little in that small classroom.

What I really wanted to cut apart was myself, was you, as we used to be.

You for ordering me to do things that were wrong.

You for never opening your heart to me.

You for continuing to deny me.

I want to cut you into ribbons with a knife.

I want to cut at you until your white face is bloody, until marks are carved all over your skin, until the flesh beneath is weeping pulp.

I want to cut off your legs, your arms, your hands, your fingers. I want to peel off your skin.

Then maybe I would be at peace at last.

Can I go to where you are, Mother?

<hr/>

While Akutagawa was being treated in the hospital, Tohko and I waited with Ayame on a sofa in the lobby.

"Thank you. I'm so glad you two were there."

Ayame's face was pale.

All I'd done was call the taxi; Tohko had been the one to wrap Akutagawa's arm in a towel and stop the bleeding and to force him into the car.

"I wonder what's wrong with Kazushi. I wonder what's happened to him —," Ayame whispered hoarsely. "He's always been a good student and always been much more serious than we were. He never argued with our parents, and we never argued among ourselves. But now he's..."

Tohko gently asked, "Something seems to be bothering Akutagawa. Do any of you have any idea what?"

Ayame's pretty face, which so resembled Akutagawa's, twisted up, and she looked like she was about to cry.

"If anything was bothering him, Kazushi never...told us or asked us for help."

Her voice was sad. Tohko's face fell, too.

"Do you know who this Kanomata he mentioned is?"

Ayame's shoulders trembled at that question. Her dewy eyes became unsettled.

"If you don't mind, could you tell us about it?" Tohko urged, and Ayame began whispering in a small voice.

"Kanomata was a girl in Kazushi's fifth-grade class. But in the second term, something happened and she changed schools."

"What happened?"

Ayame searched for the words, seeming to find it difficult to speak about.

"She was bullied terribly by her classmates. They would cut up her textbooks or her gym clothes...and then during art class, she cut one of the kids who was bullying her with a chisel."

A chisel?!

I gasped. Tohko's eyes widened, too.

Ayame bent her head and tensed her hands, which she kept folded in her lap, with the pain of the memory.

"Kanomata changed schools right after that, but...that day the teacher told Kazushi in front of everyone, 'It's your fault this happened.' He didn't tell any of us about it, so when we heard it from someone else much later, we were shocked. That person's little brother had been in Kazushi's class."

"What did the teacher mean, it was all Akutagawa's fault?"

"...I don't know." Ayame shook her head. "I heard that Kanomata started getting bullied because Kazushi lied to the teacher, but...it was more than six months after it happened, and I've never been able to ask Kazushi about it. And then right after all that happened, our mother was hospitalized. Her health had been in decline for a while, and she'd been in and out of hospitals, but this time they didn't know when she'd be able to go home, and..."

Ayame's voice grew fainter and fainter.

"I guess Kazushi thought it was his fault that Mom was so sick.

Because her health started to deteriorate after she gave birth to him. He tried not to cause any problems for her, and he learned to do everything on his own and never revealed his problems to anyone."

My chest... It felt so tight.

The Akutagawa I knew was a top student, serious, always serene, and a great guy that everyone trusted. Had Akutagawa made himself that way on purpose for his mother?

"So after the teacher said that to him, and then Mom went into the hospital for so long, I think Kazushi had a really hard time with it. But all of us had our hands full with Mom and our own lives, so we didn't have time to worry about Kazushi. He was very mature back then, but he was still only an eleven-year-old boy in fifth grade."

I could see in Ayame's drooping expression how sorry she felt for what had happened to her little brother. My chest hurt even more, and my throat tightened.

I couldn't hear any more of this.

An insidious anxiety spread through my heart.

Once I heard the story, I could never pretend that I hadn't.

"When I heard that Kazushi had slashed someone with a chisel, it reminded me of the incident in elementary school. And when Kazushi said Kanomata's name today, I felt like I was being hit over the head... It's been affecting him this whole time, I just know it."

Tohko drooped. She heard Ayame out with a pained look on her face.

Just then, Akutagawa returned, a bandage wrapped around his arm.

"Kazushi!"

Ayame ran over to him.

Akutagawa's face was unnaturally still.

"Sorry to worry you. The cuts weren't serious. They said they'd heal soon."

Ayame's voice broke at how calm he was. "I can't believe you —
you're supposed to be an honor student. How can you just say
sorry for that? I just — I can't —"

As Ayame started crying, Akutagawa put an arm around her
gently. Even though Akutagawa had been the one to cause all the
commotion and had been taken to the hospital, it was as if their
positions were reversed. His arm still around Ayame's shoulders,
he bowed his head to us.

"I put you two to a lot of trouble, as well. The school still hasn't
decided what they want to do, and things are kind of hectic right
now. Could we talk again some other time?"

His detachment felt like an oblique rejection.

Surprisingly, Tohko withdrew quietly.

She looked up at Akutagawa and smiled coolly.

"All right. But if anything's bothering you or has you feeling cornered, you'll say so, right? Konoha and I both want to help you."

It was impossible for me to chime in, so I turned my gaze down
subtly and said nothing.

When we left the hospital, it was completely dark outside and a
cool breeze blew, stabbing at the skin.

We stood together at a bus stop and waited for the bus.

After the silence had gone on for a minute or two, Tohko said,
"I want to investigate what happened with Kanomata. What
drove Akutagawa to this point, what it is that's bothering him,
and the library books being cut up and Akutagawa cutting Igarashi with a chisel — I get the feeling it's all tied to that event."

"I'm against it. You would just be meddling. We don't have any
right to dig up other people's secrets."

Tohko looked a little sad.

"You're always like that, Konoha. But Akutagawa isn't 'other
people'; he's your friend."

Suddenly she seemed on the verge of yelling at me.

But that was just her opinion! Akutagawa wasn't my friend! I would never make another friend ever again!

But if I said that, I knew Tohko would look at me even more sadly. When I'd first joined the book club in first year, she would occasionally look at me like that, and I just couldn't handle it.

Faced with my silence, her expression turned resolute.

"We've come too far to turn back now, so it's too late for regrets. If you don't want to do it, then I'll go to Akutagawa's old elementary school by myself."

———⊰⬦⊱———

This letter is my warning to you.

You have to get away, please.

Every time you rest your sweet, poison-laden hands on my heart, you send it reeling and my spirit thrums crazily. I can't control the destructive impulses that surge through me.

I tremble with a desire to cut you apart. When I close my eyes, all I see — night or day — is you.

I yearn to cut your spiteful gaze apart — that pale, dignified face you turn on me, your slender, arrogant throat — to carve away your ears and nose, to dig your eyeballs out of your head. My heart cries out to etch a crucifix into your supple chest and to paint your entire body in fountains of warm blood.

You have to get away.

I know I'll cut you apart.

———⊰⬦⊱———

In the end, I was close behind Tohko when she went to Akutagawa's old school after classes on Friday.

When Tohko said, "I'll go by myself," it was as good as a threat. I could hardly let a reckless person like her go off alone.

At the reception desk, Tohko declared with an easy smile, "I'm a graduate. I'd like to look around." We changed into slippers and walked right in.

It looked like the students were in the middle of a drawing contest for autumn or something, the walls all decorated with drawings by them. The winning pictures had gold bits of paper stuck on them.

"Let's go to the teachers' lounge first. There should still be some teachers around from back then," said Tohko.

"Do you think they'll talk about bullying to outsiders?"

"That's where you have to be totally sincere and knock them off their feet."

Tohko made a fist.

Then she saw the drawings on the wall, and her expression softened instantly.

"Isn't this nostalgic? Now I want to go back to my old elementary school. Hey Konoha, what were you like in elementary school?"

"Normal. I played very seriously with clay during art class and cut up drawing paper and fed the goldfish our class kept when I was in charge of the animals."

I remembered that I'd also met Miu in elementary school.

Miu had transferred into my class in third grade.

"I hate the way the teachers say my name. Just call me Miu. And I'll just call you Konoha."

"But everyone will make fun of us."

"Are you afraid of them? You're such a scaredy-cat. Don't call me that then if you don't wanna."

115

"No, I will. I'll call you Miu."

The image of Miu and I when we were little, running down the hall hand in hand, rose like a mirage, and I felt dizzy.

Hiding how disturbed I felt, I asked in return, "I bet you were totally rambunctious and gave your parents and teachers all kinds of trouble, right, Tohko?"

She gave me an unexpectedly serious answer.

"Until about third grade, I was a shy, quiet little girl. It's true. Lunchtime was so depressing. I hated it. Even now when I think about going to school and having to eat lunch, my stomach starts to hurt."

My mouth eagerly awaited the opportunity to put in a dig, but I closed it again without a word.

Tohko couldn't experience the taste of the food you and I normally eat.

Even the flavors of the books that she relates so rapturously are nothing but Tohko's imagination, switched out for the flavors we know.

I wasn't sure a girl in elementary school would be able to deal with that.

She wouldn't pick up on the taste of the stew or the pudding that everyone said was so delicious. It would have no taste at all. I wondered how Tohko had felt when she discovered that.

Tohko smiled gently.

"But when I went home, my mother was waiting for me at the door. She would ask me, 'Did you eat all your lunch? Good job! What a good girl!' and she would stroke my hair and write me sweet treats. Her treats were...so good. My father and I loved the meals she wrote for us."

Tohko was staying with friends of her family. Where were her mom and dad? And from what she'd just said, it sounded like her dad also ate paper like she did. What must their family be like?

Then Tohko's eyes suddenly began glinting, and she went into a second-grade classroom.

I went after her, wondering what she was doing, then saw the children's books lined up on the small wooden bookshelf. She was rejoicing.

"Look at this, Konoha! They're readers! Oh, I used to love these. They have a digest version of *Les Misérables*. This one ends when Valjean and Cosette start living happily ever after. When I read the complete version, I was blown away when that happened to Valjean. Ohhh, and they have *Little Women*. I love the scene where they deliver treats on Christmas. I read it so many times. Oh, and *My Father's Dragon* and *The Haveybavey Tree,* too! I *loved* those! I *wish* I could eat them!"

"You *do* remember why we came here, right?!"

My voice was more aggressive than I meant it to be.

Tohko was still hugging the class's copy of *The Haveybavey Tree,* but she half hid her face behind it and quieted down.

"I'm sorry. I got carried away," she said, slumping and looking vulnerably up at me. Then she pulled the book away from her face and shouted, her eyes wide, "I got it, Konoha!"

"Got what?"

"All the books that were cut up! I think they might have all been stories from textbooks!"

With that, she lost herself in the explanation.

"There was *Owl Moon* by Jane Yolen, right? I read Ju Mukuhato's 'Old Daizo and the Gun,' Sakyo Komatsu's 'Alien Homework,' and Hakushū Kitahara's 'Ancient Murrelet' in my elementary school language arts book, and Takeo Arishima's 'A Bunch of Grapes' and Sachio Ito's *Tomb of the Wild Chrysanthemum* were assigned reading over the summer. Yeah, I'm sure it was for fifth grade."

When she listed off the titles like that, they sounded familiar to me, too. Wasn't *Owl Moon* the story of a girl who goes searching for an owl with her father on a winter night?

"You mean the books at the library weren't being cut up at random?"

"That's what that would mean. But why cut up the books?"

Tohko pressed a finger to her lip and was just sinking into thought when —

"What are you two doing?"

I jumped.

A woman of around fifty held a binder to her chest, looking at us suspiciously.

"S-sorry. Um, we're...well —"

Tohko swept in front of me as I grew flustered.

Her expression was the very image of seriousness, and the teacher gasped. Tohko took another step toward her, then suddenly launched into her eloquent explanation.

"We are the classmates and mentors of Kazushi Akutagawa, who used to go to school here. We came to ask something very important about Kazushi. Please, it's very urgent! Could you help us out?"

Whether it was Tohko's fervent appeal that moved the heart of the woman who was dedicated to education, or whether her honor student–like conduct had a greater effect...

We were taken through the teachers' offices and into a small room with a nameplate on it, where we were seated on a sofa and allowed to hear the story.

Mrs. Yamamura, who Tohko inspired to talk without restraint, had been Akutagawa's teacher twice, and she remembered the incident clearly.

"His teacher at the time was Yuka Momoki. She was an intense young teacher, but that meant she had excessive expectations of her students. I don't think she could accept that a child in her class was being bullied or that she would stab one of her classmates with a chisel. No matter what reason Ms. Momoki had for saying such a thing to Akutagawa at the time, it was an awful thing for a teacher to do. Ms. Momoki realized that and deeply regretted it...Apparently she tried to apologize to him later on, but once she'd said it, it couldn't be taken back. She must have felt that she had failed as a teacher. She left the school soon after."

"Why did Ms. Momoki blame Akutagawa? What had he done?" Tohko asked.

Her face dark, Mrs. Yamamura whispered, "He told Ms. Momoki that a classmate was being bullied.

"It was the natural thing for him to do since he was the class monitor. He hadn't done anything worthy of blame. But in fact there was no bullying. The child who was suspected of bullying got angry anyway, and then the bullying truly started. That child led the rest until half the class was ignoring that one girl or hiding her things or deliberately tripping her."

Mrs. Yamamura's every word landed heavily on my heart.

Akutagawa wasn't at fault.

But if I had been in his place — if because of something I had said, someone started getting picked on and the teacher blamed me for it — I would probably feel like I was being cut apart by icy blades. This would probably deepen into a wound I would remember forever.

Tohko looked sad as well.

Mrs. Yamamura sighed.

"Kanomata, the girl who was being bullied, and Akutagawa were good friends, and they often studied together in the library. Kanomata was a child who was often alone, but I remember that Akutagawa was the only one with whom she seemed to enjoy talking. So he must have had an extra hard time of it."

"Kanomata still hasn't forgiven me!" I remembered Akutagawa shouting, his face twisted and covered in blood. My throat tightened.

"That's all I can tell you about it. I hope it's at least some help to Akutagawa."

"Thank you very much. Do you happen to have any pictures of their class that we could look at?" asked Tohko.

Mrs. Yamamura seemed to hesitate, but then she whispered, "Just a moment," and stood up. She brought back a bundle of newspapers tied up with string from a shelf at the back of the room.

They looked like monthly papers printed by the school and were about half the size of normal newspapers. She flipped through them, then stopped.

"This is a picture of fifth-grade class three."

It looked like a group photo from a field trip with all the children lined up in front of a tour bus holding their bags. It looked to be roughly the same time of year as right now. Everyone had a knitted vest or a cardigan over their long-sleeved shirts.

"This is Akutagawa."

She pointed out a tall, handsome boy on the leftmost edge of the picture.

She slid her finger to the next child over.

"And this is Kanomata."

When I saw the quiet-looking girl with long hair, I started.

Something about her reminded me of Sarashina. Her hairstyle or her demeanor or...

And that wasn't all. There was a familiar-looking rabbit doll dangling from the bag she carried.

A pale pink rabbit.

It looked like the rabbit lying on the floor of Akutagawa's room with its head and limbs cut off. No — I was sure I'd seen it somewhere before that...

"My rabbit is missing."

"What?"

"The one I bought when we all went to that store with Tohko. Oh no. Did I lose it somewhere?"

Right! It was the rabbit Kotobuki had on her bag!

As soon as I realized that, a new question chilled my heart. Could the rabbit in Akutagawa's room have belonged to Kotobuki?!

If that was true, maybe he'd picked it up somewhere and taken it home, not realizing it was hers.

Still looking at the photograph, Tohko placed a white finger on a girl standing at the rightmost edge.

"Who is this?"

I almost shouted again.

It was a girl with short hair and a cold expression. Her lips pressed together irritably, the girl had a bag slung over her shoulder, and dangling from it was the same pink rabbit as Kanomata's.

Cold sweat rolled down my back. Could this really be a coincidence?

Mrs. Yamamura's face tensed instantly at Tohko's question.

She seemed to find it difficult to tell us the short-haired girl's name.

"…That's Konishi. Has she done something?"

"No. She has the same rabbit doll as Kanomata, so I thought maybe they were friends."

"Well, they may have been. Though Kanomata didn't seem to have any friends other than Akutagawa. Maybe this rabbit was simply popular among the girls," she offered evasively, then closed the paper.

"What do you think, Konoha?" Tohko whispered as we walked to the school gate. "I wonder if it's just a coincidence that

Kanomata and Konishi had the same rabbit doll. And Mrs. Yamamura was acting a little strangely. She didn't seem to want to tell us about Konishi."

"I got that feeling, too."

Tohko stopped in her tracks and looked at me with her clear, black eyes.

"I think Konishi might have been the one who was bullying Kanomata."

———◆———

Were you the one who said that it was a mistake to have met then? Or did I say it first?

In any case, we felt the same way about that at least, and we had the same regrets and the same pain.

When we were little, the things we promised each other were nothing but vague phantoms, and it was a foolish delusion to think that when our eyes met our hearts were linked.

What we were looking at was only ourselves in the end, and we didn't have the slightest understanding about who the other person was — about what secrets they hid inside themselves. Nor...

The truth about the monsters hidden inside us.

Even now we carry the same suffering.

That is the one thing that brings us together.

But your dark desires drive me away.

Mother, I want to be at peace.

———◆———

I spent Sunday at home playing with Maika.

"Again, Konoha!" she pleaded, so we kept playing the fighting game on the TV. Watching Maika as her big, unsullied eyes darted around and she cheered or laughed, I felt strange. Had I been this innocent when I was a child?

Would I have been able to go on having a strong, pure heart, never doubting or fearing others, if I hadn't met Miu?

I felt like each time people failed, they became cowards and grew dirtier.

And in elementary school, Akutagawa had failed spectacularly. He was still suffering from those memories.

I was unable to breathe whenever I remembered Miu, and he still felt remorse about Kanomata. He and I were a lot alike, I thought bitterly.

"See you tonight."

The next morning—Monday—I was supposed to meet up with Tohko in the club room, so I left home early.

On the way home from visiting Akutagawa's old school, Tohko had been pretty hung up on the rabbit dolls that Kanomata and Konishi had on their bags.

When I told her about Kotobuki's rabbit, her eyes had grown thoughtful.

"I see...Nanase's rabbit disappeared?"

"There was a cut-up rabbit doll lying in Akutagawa's room, remember."

"You're right..."

After a brief silence, Tohko had pressed a finger to her lip and said, still deep in thought, "That bunny is from a popular line of products, and the different colors have different meanings."

"Different meanings?"

"As in, red is for good grades, yellow is for luck with money, blue is for luck with friends."

"What's pink?"

"Luck in love. They say if you keep the rabbit nearby, the person you like will start to feel the same way. So pink is the most popular color."

I was shocked that Kotobuki was worried about luck in love. She usually acted like she couldn't care less about boys.

On the other hand, the fact that Kanomata and Konishi had the same good luck charm only deepened the mystery.

Tohko had talked about the possibility that Konishi was the one who had bullied Kanomata.

If so, wouldn't the relationships between Akutagawa, Kanomata, and Konishi involve even more pain?

Why had Konishi bullied Kanomata? The root cause of that would—

"I still don't think Akutagawa was the one who cut up the library books or the one who hurt Igarashi. But if that's true..."

Tohko fell utterly silent. I could tell what she was thinking, and I felt anxious, as if I was standing in murky darkness.

When we parted ways, Tohko said, *"On Monday morning before homeroom starts, come to the book club room. I'll look into the things that are still bothering me before that."*

As I walked along my usual route to school, a late autumn breeze pricked at my skin. I was drinking in the clear sunlight when I spotted Akutagawa standing in front of a mailbox.

He was wearing his school uniform. His bike was parked beside him, and he stood with his back straight, looking down at a long white envelope in his hands.

Angst clouded his strong, handsome profile, and the gaze he fixed on the envelope was so bereft and sad that it pained me.

Don't go over there.

Don't call out to him.

I told myself desperately, my jaw tight, biting down on my lip.

But my feet carried me toward him, as if drawn there.

I knew it was because I'd listened to Ayame and Mrs. Yamamura.

"Akutagawa?" I whispered almost inaudibly, and he started and looked at me, still holding the envelope.

"...Inoue."

I couldn't manage a smile. Looking uncomfortable, I asked, "They let you come back to school, huh?"

Akutagawa's face was hard, too.

"Yeah...for now."

"That's good."

The silence drew out. Hesitantly, Akutagawa opened his mouth to speak.

"Sorry about before. It's too bad you and Amano had to come all that way."

"That's okay. How's your arm?"

"Almost healed. I can even get in the tub, as long as I keep my arm out."

"Yeah?"

Silence again.

This time I was the one to break it.

"Um..."

Akutagawa watched me morosely.

"Those letters —" I forced my voice out, though it caught in my throat. "I see you mailing them a lot. Who are you sending them to?"

Akutagawa's gaze shifted slightly away.

Pain shot through my belly as the silence drew out.

"Did your family ask you to send something again?" I asked feebly, but then Akutagawa let out a sigh.

"No, they're my letters. That other one was, too."

125

He turned his broad back to me and quietly dropped the envelope into the mailbox.

Then he turned back around, and his face calm but somehow morose, he said, "Would you walk with me for a little bit, Inoue?"

Chapter 5 – You Were Crying That Day

He took me to the general hospital where Kotobuki had stayed that summer.

Akutagawa walked slowly down the white hallways that smelled of medicine.

So far, he had barely said a word. I'd stayed silent as well.

We went into a private room, where a petite woman, who looked to be in her midthirties, lay in a bed.

Her mouth and body were hooked up to several machines via tubes. Her eyes stayed closed, and she didn't move.

Akutagawa looked down at the woman, then let out a breath and said, "This is my mom. She's been in the hospital like this ever since I was eleven."

A shock stabbed my heart.

She'd been like this ever since Akutagawa was eleven?! Without ever waking up?

I remembered how difficult it had been for Ayame to talk about.

"And then right after all that happened, our mother was hospitalized. Her health had been in decline for a while, and she'd been in and out of hospitals, but this time they didn't know when she'd be able to go home, and..."

They didn't know when she would be released...I had no idea that this is what she'd meant.

There was a basket filled with oranges and grapefruits on the table beside her bed, which gave off a tangy fragrance.

Beside that was a stack of unopened long white envelopes. At a quick glance, I counted more than ten.

They were addressed to Yoshiko Akutagawa, care of the hospital. When I saw that, I realized who Akutagawa had been sending his letters to, and I felt my throat quivering. I thought I might cry.

Akutagawa picked up one of the envelopes. His downcast eyes fell sadly on the recipient's name.

"I knew she would never read these letters, no matter how many I sent...but that just meant that when I couldn't control my feelings anymore, I could purge them into a letter. Then I felt compelled to send it. That made me feel like she had accepted the burden for me, and I could relax again."

He sounded detached, speaking almost in a whisper, and the very calmness of his voice filled it with sorrow.

"Giving birth to me wrecked my mom's health, but she never blamed me for it. She always smiled at me."

Ayame told us that Akutagawa had always done everything for himself ever since he was little. She said he'd been that way so that he wouldn't cause his mother any trouble.

Akutagawa put the letter back on the table and turned his gaze to his mother once more.

He had a faintly despondent look, his profile charged with sorrow.

"Of all the people in the world, my mother would probably be the only one to forgive me, no matter how despicable the feelings in my heart. So she's the one person I can't lie to. I've always written down how I truly felt in these letters."

"But all of us had our hands full with Mom and our own lives, so we didn't have time to worry about Kazushi."

"He was very mature back then, but he was still only an eleven-year-old boy in fifth grade."

Had Akutagawa written a letter about the incident six years ago? And what about this latest incident?

Akutagawa picked up one of the oranges from the basket and offered it to me.
"Let's go outside."
"Okay."
I accepted the orange and nodded awkwardly.

We sat side by side on a bench in the hospital's garden, and while we ate the slightly bitter oranges, I revealed that Tohko and I had gone to his elementary school.
"I'm sorry. I know you told us not to get involved."
Akutagawa wasn't very surprised. He bit into an orange segment before quietly saying, "It's fine... There was something wrong with me when I cut my arm. I couldn't fight the impulse to cut everything apart and put an end to it."
"Why did you say 'Kanomata still hasn't forgiven me'?" I asked timidly.
Akutagawa's face went dark as he answered, his thick fingers peeling the skin from a second orange.

"After what happened, Kanomata started to take on a new life inside me. She's still the same age, and sometimes she'll talk to me. 'Why did you break your promise? If you hadn't betrayed me, things never would have gotten so bad. No one would have suffered. My pain is going to last forever.'"

I felt as if I could hear Kanomata's voice in my ears, though I had never met her, and a shudder ran down my spine.

"What did you promise her? What...*happened* six years ago? Why did you think Kanomata was getting bullied?"

"Because her textbooks and notes were being cut to shreds. All the time."

He stopped peeling the orange and started to tell me about what had happened six years earlier.

How his desk ended up next to hers when they changed the seating arrangement in the second term; how he had glanced over at her desk during language arts class, and Kanomata was on the verge of tears looking down at her textbook, its pages sliced up in every direction.

She noticed him looking and quickly closed her book, and during the break, she told him over and over, "Don't tell anyone about this. I don't want the teacher to know, either."

But after that, her things kept getting cut up.

The slash of a box cutter running across her pen case, the number cut off her gym clothes, her pencil board with the picture of a cute character on it; a light blue hand towel — every time Akutagawa discovered something, Kanomata's face twisted with tears and he would push it back into secrecy out of embarrassment.

She had pleaded to Akutagawa, "Don't tell anyone. I want to keep it a secret."

Akutagawa was torn over whether he should protect Kanomata's secret or whether he should get help from the teacher. But

Kanomata had begged him so frantically that he'd been unable to break his promise. Instead, he worried for her and told her to keep her things in his locker and brought her his sister's old textbook.

Kanomata grew to rely on Akutagawa, and the two wound up becoming friends.

"I think Kanomata didn't get along very well with her parents. Her father was a stern professional, and she talked all the time about how he would scold her pretty badly if her grades dropped and how stifling it was. She hated her name, too. It was Emi, as in 'smile.'"

"They told me that when I was born, the mountains were smiling. I never understand what my dad is talking about. I hate the name Emi. I can't even smile in front of my parents."

Kanomata would occasionally give voice to startling opinions like that. She was a girl with a strong heart in contrast to her quiet exterior. After school, she and Akutagawa would pass the time doing homework in the library or reading books.

"My favorite story in the textbook is Ryunosuke Akutagawa's story 'Tangerines.' I mean, his name is Akutagawa!"

"Hey—you're on my side, right, Akutagawa? We'll be friends forever, right?"

"In fact, I remember now that I ate oranges with Kanomata like this, too. I think it was during a field trip."

Akutagawa's eyes grew distant.

"She was a very important friend to me even though she was a girl."

The conflict over whether he should tell the teacher or protect his promise to his friend raged on all that time inside him.

And then one day, Akutagawa saw his classmate Konishi yelling at Kanomata. Kanomata had tears in her eyes, but she was taking it. Konishi had often glared at the two of them, so Akutagawa wondered if maybe Konishi was the one who'd been bothering Kanomata.

When he asked Kanomata if she was fighting with Konishi, Kanomata's face tensed with fear and she didn't say anything, so his suspicion of Konishi only deepened.

Around that time, Kanomata kept her books and notes in Akutagawa's desk, but one day as Akutagawa was handing her the old textbook, they saw that the cover had been all cut up. Kanomata couldn't take it any longer.

Tears rolled down her cheeks, and she hugged the book to her chest. "I'm sorry...You gave me this and everything. I'm really sorry. Really."

After seeing that, Akutagawa told their teacher Ms. Momoki that Kanomata was the victim of anonymous bullying.

Ms. Momoki called Konishi in and asked her what was going on. Konishi stayed ruefully quiet, and when the teacher told her, "You can be friends with Kanomata, can't you?" Konishi nodded, but she had begun to tremble. Then the teacher said, "Now things will be better."

"Konishi hadn't been bullying Kanomata at all. No one in the class had."

Akutagawa hung his head bitterly.
"Kanomata was the one cutting up her own books."
I gasped.
"Why would she do that?"

"All I can do is guess, but maybe it was her form of rebellion against her parents. Or it might have been a silent SOS to them. A cry for help. Otherwise, it could be like me, and she couldn't control her impulse to cut something apart…

"The one thing I'm sure of is that Kanomata started to get bullied for real, because I broke my promise to her, and one day she slashed Konishi with a chisel. The incident became public, and Kanomata's father had problems at his job because of it, so she switched schools. Ms. Momoki stopped teaching, too. Everyone's lives were destroyed by my rash actions."

"It's your fault!"

I imagined how he must have felt when the teacher berated him in class, and I thought my chest might rip open. All Akutagawa had done was to be unable to turn his back on Kanomata when she cried. But instead that had driven her away.

Kanomata still lived on in Akutagawa's heart unchanged, and she still blamed him.

The orange he had been eating lay forgotten in his hand. Akutagawa bit down on his lip with a hard expression.

I gently asked, "This might sound strange, but you know that pink rabbit in your room? What was that?"

"That rabbit," Akutagawa murmured, sounding exhausted, "was a birthday gift. I was too self-conscious to go into a girlie store by myself, so I went with Kanomata and she picked it out. She said she liked that one… But after she transferred, she sent it back to me, along with 'Tangerines.'"

"Tangerines?"

He looked up at my question and smiled sadly.

"'Tangerines' by Ryunosuke Akutagawa, the story from the textbook. She cut it out of the book and sent it to me with the

133

rabbit, whose head she'd cut off. She probably couldn't stand to see the name Akutagawa anymore."

"That's—"

My throat tightened and choked off my voice.

It was too awful. Akutagawa hadn't done anything wrong.

His eyes were still cast down.

"After that, my mom got the way she is now, and I felt like I was being punished. Ever since then, I've tried to act cautiously, to be an honorable, intelligent person so that I would never hurt anyone again. But then I got involved in a love triangle and hurt Igarashi. I really am an awful person."

That's not true. You're not an awful person. It's not your fault. I wanted to tell him all that.

But I couldn't say it.

I was scared—

Just scared.

If I said something halfhearted just to temporarily placate him, I felt like he would yell at me again. I was so afraid of that I was practically shaking.

"Tohko says it was probably someone else who hurt Igarashi. That you're covering for them."

I was a coward. Since I couldn't say what I was feeling, I told him what Tohko had said. Even that took everything I had.

Surprise flashed over Akutagawa's features, and they finally settled into a look of powerful suffering and sadness. He clenched his fists in an effort to stop himself from trembling and said, "I was definitely the one who stabbed Igarashi. The chisel belonged to me. I did everything—all of it."

Who was he protecting? I had guessed, too, now. There weren't that many choices, and the answer had been there the whole time.

But I couldn't guess his reasons. Why was Akutagawa forced to

134

martyr himself to this extent? Because of guilt about the past? Or...?

"Akutagawa — did Sarashina used to be —?"

Akutagawa tensed his jaw fiercely. He stood up, interrupting my question, and with a harsh look, he told me, "I'm tied to the past. I can't cut that bond. I intend to take full responsibility for what I did."

Then he handed me the orange he'd started eating.

"Sorry, can you finish this? I'm going to school."

Then straightening his back, he started walking.

I quickly asked, "Just let me ask one more thing, Akutagawa. Did you go out with Sarashina because you liked her? Do you like her now?"

Akutagawa turned around, and his eyes were clear and sad.

"I used to. But now, there's someone I wish I could see. And it's not her."

After he left, I sat on the bench alone and ate the rest of the orange.

I peeled the tough skin off with my fingers, took one of the segments, and put it in my mouth.

The bitter acidity prickled in my nose.

"Ahchoo!"

I heard the sneeze behind me and turned, and there was Tohko hunkered down behind a tree, hugging her knees.

"What are you doing here?!" I asked, my eyes bugging out. She stood up, picking off the grass stuck to her skirt with a reddened face; then shyly and feebly, she said, "I saw you and Akutagawa on my way to school, so...I followed you."

"Have you been eavesdropping this whole time?"

"...Sorry."

She sat down next to me and rested her hands in her lap guiltily.

"Are you angry?"

"What's done is done. I give up," I murmured quietly, peeling the skin from another orange. The truth was, I was a little relieved to see her.

"Can I...have some, too?"

"You won't be able to taste it."

"That's okay. Gimme."

I peeled off all the skin and split the last orange in halves, then gave one of them to Tohko.

"Thanks."

She broke off one segment and ate it in silence.

I ate my orange, too.

"How did that story by Ryunosuke Akutagawa go again?" I asked.

"The first-person narrator paints a beautiful, gentle, vibrant scene that he glimpses for only a moment from the train. In elementary school textbooks, all the big words are simplified.

"The narrator feels horribly irritated by an imbecilic, shabbily dressed farm girl who gets into the same compartment as him. The girl opened the window before they went into a tunnel, so the seats fill with soot and the narrator's rage reaches its peak. But once they pass through the tunnel, several little boys come to see the girl off, as she's presumably going to their master's house, and the girl tosses tangerines to them through the window, one after another.

"The tangerines bob vividly in the balmy light of the setting sun. When he sees that, the narrator feels suddenly cheerful.

"It tastes so sweet and tart and happy, it makes my chest squeeze tight. It tastes like this orange. Tart, but...it touches your heart deeply."

"Aren't oranges sweet?"

"Nope. They're sour."

She added quietly, "I think." Then her face reddened, and she ate another segment.

"You're right," I murmured back. "They are sour."

As we ate the sour orange, Tohko mumbled, "Um, remember how I said I would look into Sarashina? In fifth grade, Sarashina's parents divorced, and she switched schools. Sarashina is her mother's maiden name."

I stopped eating and hung on her words.

Sounding a little sad, Tohko said, "Sarashina's name used to be…"

⟹◆⟸

I fell in love when I saw you crying and alone.

As the sun was setting, I saw a girl arguing with her mother on the other side of some orange bushes. Her mother went into the house without paying the slightest attention to what the girl said, leaving her alone in the yard. The girl hugged her knees and curled up into a ball. Her shoulders were shaking.

She was so fragile, stifling her sobs — so different from the girl I knew that my heart ached even through my surprise. I could feel the sweet fragrance of oranges making me light-headed.

All despite the fact that I was incapable of caring for anyone the way that I was.

I want to see you.

Very much.

More than I can bear.

Though I fiercely command them not to, my feet try to go to you. I want to trust everything to you. I want to grant your every wish, to be suffused by the darkness. I would fall to any depths.

If only to feel your presence.

Only to hear your voice.

I want to see you.
I do.
But I can't see you as I am now.

——⋙◆⋘——

When we got back to school, it was lunchtime.

I had just quietly opened the door at the back of the bustling classroom and stepped inside when I heard a prickly voice behind me.

"Keeping CEO's hours? Must be nice."

When I turned around, Kotobuki was glowering at me, her arms folded over her chest and her lips pursed.

"Ack!"

"What's that for?" she asked.

"You just scared me, talking to me out of nowhere like that. Good morning, Kotobuki."

"It's not morning anymore," she snapped; then she lowered her voice.

"Akutagawa came today. He missed the first two periods, though."

"Oh? Well that's something," I murmured, pretending not to know anything.

"He's in the teacher's office right now, but he was real calm and said hi to everyone. He seemed like he was in a good mood."

Her tone was brusque, but I knew Kotobuki must have been worried about Akutagawa.

She'd kept her face turned firmly away but suddenly looked at me, her expression growing uneasy. "Sarashina came back to school today, too. She came by here earlier. But Akutagawa wasn't here, so she left again. She said she was bringing him something he'd forgotten, and she was at his desk..."

At that point, Akutagawa came back.

He came through the door at the opposite end of the class from where we stood and went to his desk. When girls called out to him, he smiled softly and spoke a word or two in response. Then he sat down and started to pull his textbook and notes out to get ready for the next class when...

His face tensed immediately.

His eyes widened, his gaze fixed on his paralyzed hands. What did he see? I walked over to him.

Once I was beside Akutagawa, I discovered what it was that had surprised him so badly, and I shuddered, as if I had been splashed with cold water.

It was a fifth-grade language arts textbook.

Several cuts ran across the book's cover. His hands shaking, Akutagawa turned the book over. Written along the bottom in Magic Marker was the name Ayame Akutagawa, and beside it was a sticker on which another name had been written.

Emi Kanomata.

Akutagawa stared at the book in shock.

There was no mistaking it: It was the book he had given to Kanomata, which had once belonged to his older sister; the one from which Ryunosuke Akutagawa's story "Tangerines" had been cut and sent to his house after the incident.

Sarashina had come to drop off something Akutagawa had forgotten. That's what Kotobuki had said.

Sarashina had left the book Akutagawa had given to Kanomata inside his desk!

As he looked down at the cut-up textbook, Akutagawa didn't so much as blink. He seemed to have forgotten that he was in a classroom.

I left the room quickly.

When I heard Kotobuki gasp, I was running down the hall.

I wasn't Akutagawa's friend.

I had known not to get involved in his problems. I had already trespassed on so many boundaries. I couldn't do it again!

But Akutagawa was hurt pretty badly, and he was suffering.

Hadn't he suffered enough?

Just free him already, Konoha.

I went to class three's room, but Sarashina wasn't there.

My rising fever didn't break, and I didn't go back to my class. I ran down the stairs and cut through the school yard to look in the animal shed where the rabbits were kept. But Sarashina wasn't there, either.

Next, I went to the library. The end of lunchtime was approaching, so students were lined up in front of the checkout counter, and the one girl staffing it was working in a frenzy.

Going against the flow of the crowd, I moved deeper inside the library.

When I got to the area with the Japanese literature books, I saw Sarashina standing in front of the shelf where Akutagawa had been cutting up a book before.

Her head was bent, and she looked like she was typing out a message on her cell phone. A hardcover book — a collection of stories by Ryunosuke Akutagawa — and two pages that had been cut out of it lay on the floor. She was completely absorbed in typing her message and never made a move to pick them up.

She stared at the cell phone's screen with bloodshot eyes, panting unevenly as her fingers continued leaping around. She looked possessed. I felt cold sweat run down my back.

The bell rang announcing the end of the break, and I heard the voices and footsteps of people hurrying out of the library. The sounds moved off into the distance.

But Sarashina acted as if she hadn't heard a thing, her fingers still moving.

The area around us grew utterly silent.

In a trembling voice, I asked, "Are you texting Akutagawa?"

Sarashina jerked her head up in surprise.

"Are you going to get him to come and cover for you again?"

After a moment of hesitation, a pretty smile unbecoming to this scene came over her face.

"Kazushi is on my side, you know. He comes running whenever I'm in trouble. He's my own personal knight. Kazushi and I are bound by fate."

Her relaxed tone and happy smile gave me goose bumps. What was she saying?

"The person who stole the rabbits from the biology club and the person who cut Igarashi with the chisel ... was that you, too?"

Sarashina's face wrinkled in displeasure.

"Yes. I hate rabbits. And Igarashi was getting in my way. He was punching Kazushi and kicking him ... I couldn't forgive him for that. So I cut him with this."

She slipped her cell phone into the pocket of her skirt and drew out in its place something long and thin. When I registered that it was a chisel with a notched tip, I gulped.

"Swish —" Sarashina made a diagonal sweep through the air with the chisel, and her lips stretched into a grin. "Igarashi was so surprised. Before he fell down, his face was in total disbelief and he was blubbering. It felt great."

I felt my throat fluttering with fear. How could she say such terrible things so calmly with such unclouded, joyful eyes? Hadn't she been screaming and in tears when it happened? Had it been an act? Or did she not know what she was saying and doing?

Standing there in front of me, she looked like a dangerous, unstable creature. It was impossible to tell what she might do.

The library was blanketed in silence. Everyone must have left.

"You were…going out with Igarashi…weren't you?" I asked in a broken whisper. A look of violent rage suddenly came over Sarashina's face.

"He just decided that! No one asked me! I hate him! He's just a huge meathead, and he's shallow and self-entitled and talks in a really loud voice no matter where he is! He grins like an idiot! He jokes around! The movies we'd go see, the restaurants we went to, the food—he decided everything without asking me, and he tried to make disgusting moves on me! Every time he brazenly tried to touch my shoulder or my hand, I wanted to slice his hand up like a carrot! I don't even want to breathe the same air as him!!!"

Her voice was wild, as if every word were a stone with which she could pelt the object of her hatred. I was frozen in terror, intimidated by her glinting eyes and the chisel she still held in her hand.

"I hate him! Hate him! *Hate him!* I never want to lay eyes on him again! He bullied Kazushi! He did horrible things to him! And then he said we should go out again anyway—it made me sick! What does he mean *again*? I was never your girlfriend! Don't you get that? Idiot! I hope you die!"

Loathing, pain, suffering, rage—Sarashina's expressions changed with dizzying speed, her body trembling.

Suddenly, Akutagawa's voice sounded behind her.

"Cut it out! Don't say another word about Igarashi! Don't slander him!"

"I knew you'd come, Kazushi."

Sarashina smiled at him as if they were meeting up for a date. Akutagawa stood before her, out of breath, his face twisted with pain. Then he forced out a pleading voice, saying, "Igarashi was a great guy. He was cheerful, and he looked out for me, and everyone on the team adored him. Even when I was the only first-year chosen to be a full member of the team and the rest of the upperclassmen didn't look very happy about it, Igarashi was the only one who was truly glad for me. He patted me on the back and told me to do my best."

Akutagawa's voice was hoarse.

"He really was a great person. So when he said he wanted me to introduce you to him, I did it. I thought you wouldn't mind him. You always smiled so happily when you were with him. Don't deny it."

The smile slid off Sarashina's face.

Akutagawa continued talking, his face fighting back pain.

"I—I thought you two were getting along. I was relieved. But then you lied and told me he'd hit you and was stalking you... You tricked me."

"You tricked me first!" Sarashina shouted, her eyes timid now. "When you asked me to come watch a match, I was so happy. I went to watch lots of matches after that, and you came to talk to me every time. Igarashi was always with you, but I only cared about you, so I was okay with that.

"I thought we were getting closer, and I was so happy, and then when you invited me to an amusement park, I was overjoyed! Igarashi was with us, but I was happier than I'd ever been because it was the weekend, and I was going out with you.

"So whenever you invited me somewhere, I dressed up super-nice and would go to the place we were supposed to meet ten minutes early, my heart pounding the whole time. But then in the middle of it, you would say that something urgent had come up or that you'd caught a cold, and you'd cancel at the last minute, and somehow that made me Igarashi's girlfriend!"

Akutagawa didn't answer. He let Sarashina talk, his lips pressed tightly together and his brow knit.

I felt as if my heart was on fire. Akutagawa hadn't meant to deceive her. He had probably just fixed up a girl from his class with the upperclassman he respected so much as a favor to the guy.

The way Omiya had supported the match between Sugiko and his best friend Nojima.

But just as Sugiko had preferred Omiya, Sarashina's heart was not with Igarashi: It had fixed instead on Akutagawa.

"I knew you were friends with Igarashi, so I put up with him that whole time because I didn't want you to hate me. But going out to eat or see movies alone with him was pure torture for me. Gradually, just the sound of his laughter set my teeth on edge, and when I couldn't stand it any longer, I told you so. Sure, Igarashi never hit me or anything, but he might as well have!"

Sarashina gripped the chisel in both hands, then pulled it close to her own chest and retreated a step, a look of heartrending sorrow on her face.

"I managed to break up with Igarashi, and you became my boyfriend, and we were finally happy. So why did you say we should break up, Kazushi? Because I stabbed Igarashi? *Kanomata made me do that.* She was threatening to take you away if I didn't. I didn't want to do anything that would make you hate me. But—but—I hated Igarashi, and Kanomata...that day she...When the blood splattered on me, she laughed that she had gotten her revenge...that she wanted me to get hurt, too, so...so it's not my fault!"

The blade was against Sarashina's throat.

His face ashen, Akutagawa groaned. "Give me the chisel."

"No!!!" Sarashina screamed. *"Answer me!* Why did you break up with me? It's almost my birthday! So why? Why did you do it?!"

Akutagawa approached Sarashina slowly, forcing out a pained

voice. "I thought that was what we agreed in the first place. You wanted me to pretend to be your boyfriend because you hated having Igarashi follow you around. You were terrified, so we agreed that I would take on the role of your fake boyfriend for one year. That year ended last month."

Sarashina's face morphed from a crazed expression to laughing tears.

"Sure, at first. But I never intended to just say good-bye after a year. I tried to make you notice me that whole time.

"I baked you cookies. I knitted you a scarf. I grew my hair out. I really did try my very best."

I remembered the moldy cakes and cookies scattered around Akutagawa's room and felt as if my heart was ripping open. I could imagine how Sarashina's desperate efforts had been too intense for Akutagawa, and...

"We've been a great couple and never once fought this entire year. That's true, isn't it? You must have started to like me after one year. Haven't you?"

Akutagawa couldn't answer. His face contorted even further, and he bit down on his lip.

Sarashina watched him sadly, and madness came once more over her face. Her wet eyes flashed with hatred.

"I see. Someone must have bad-mouthed me again. Like *she* did!"

The next moment, Sarashina's gaze locked onto me.

She raised the chisel over her head.

"Inoue? Did you say something mean about me to Kazushi? Were you the one who told him to break up with me?!"

"No, I—"

"Stop it, Sarashina! Inoue has nothing to do with this!"

"Answer me, Kazushi. Answer me! *Did Kanomata bad-mouth me again?!*"

146

Her scream reverberated off the walls, and the blade of the chisel glinted before my eyes. Just as she seemed ready to swing it down at me —

"Stop, Konishi!"

Sarashina froze, as if she'd been physically struck by that dignified voice.

Clopping footsteps sounded in the silent library.

Tohko walked past me, her long braids swaying like cats' tails. She planted herself in front of Sarashina.

"Why are you here?" I gaped.

Her gaze resting on Sarashina, Tohko replied, "Chia tipped me off that Sarashina was at the library."

Takeda popped out beside me.

"I was on duty at the desk today. Sarashina was acting really weird, so I went to get Tohko."

There were usually two people on duty at the desk, but now that I thought about it, there had been only one and that was why there was a line at the counter.

"Sarashina," Tohko said, "in fifth grade your name was Mayuri Konishi, from Akutagawa's class. Right?"

"How did you know that?"

At Sarashina's forbidding look, Tohko planted her right hand on her hip and crisply declared, "Because I'm a book girl!"

Sarashina just...*stared* at her.

She had a point. The only possible response to someone appearing unannounced in the midst of a bloody battle and then making an airheaded declaration like that was to either fly off the handle because you thought you were being made fun of or to stare agape because you had no idea what was happening.

Akutagawa looked at Tohko in utter perplexity, too.

Man, why did she always have to meddle in everything?

Sarashina lowered her hands to the level of her chest.

Tohko started talking without any sign of fear.

"There have been a lot of reports of cut-up books at the library recently. And as I cherish the written word with all my heart, I was seized by righteous indignation and searched for the perpetrator. Akutagawa said that he was the one who'd cut them up, but he'd only cut one book — and that was only one page out of a collection by Takeo Arishima. Of course, I still consider that an egregious crime. But he had a reason for doing it. He was covering for the one who was actually cutting up the other books. Which was you, wasn't it, Sarashina?"

Sarashina's face was still full of wonder. She must have felt like the conversation had derailed, and she couldn't follow it. In contrast, Tohko's tongue was moving at top speed.

"Even if you don't answer, I can tell from seeing the Ryunosuke Akutagawa collection at your feet and the chisel in your hand.

"All the books that were cut up are used in fifth-grade language arts textbooks.

"When Akutagawa was in fifth grade, there was a big stir when a girl in his class, who was getting bullied, brandished a chisel in class. The cut marks left on the books' pages were slightly different than those left by a box cutter. There were two vertical lines. A chisel would leave marks like that, no?

"I tested cutting paper with a chisel. It took a little bit of force, but once I got used to it, I could cut the paper neatly, and it left two lines on the page below. Meaning that the books were cut with a chisel.

"Don't you think this accumulation of coincidences is odd?

"So I imagined that the person Akutagawa was protecting was someone involved in what happened in his class and who was still in his life.

"There was only Igarashi and you, Sarashina, for him to protect.

"Igarashi's throat was slashed with a blade, and he got taken to the hospital in an ambulance. So that left only you."

I felt like my chest was being crushed as I listened to Tohko speak.

She was right. The *moment* that Akutagawa wounded Igarashi with the chisel, we had guessed who he was protecting.

That day, he'd received a text message on his cell phone and ran out of the auditorium, but there hadn't been enough time for Akutagawa, who had rushed to the back of the school yard still in his costume, to get his hands on a chisel or to argue and scuffle with Igarashi. And since Igarashi knew that Sarashina had stabbed him, he had been struck mute by his shock.

Tohko and I had both *known* in a half-formed way that Sarashina was the perpetrator.

But why had Akutagawa gone so far as to cover for her when they weren't even dating?

And why had Sarashina done those things? I hadn't understood that, and Tohko had hesitated to make any conjectures either. That was why Tohko had taken me along to the elementary school where the incident had occurred, because she believed that was the cause of it all.

Sarashina stared at Tohko, her face ashen.

"After that, all I had to do was look up your name. Your full name is Mayuri Sarashina. The name of the girl who was bullied was Emi Kanomata. And Akutagawa's older sister let me check the full name of the girl who'd bullied Kanomata on an old student register. That girl was named *Mayuri* Konishi. The same name as you, Sarashina."

I'd heard this part from Tohko while we were eating oranges at the hospital.

When we'd looked at the group photo from the field trip, I'd expected Sarashina to be revealed as Kanomata, because Sarashina now somehow resembled the Kanomata I saw in the photo, in her hairstyle or her general impression.

But Sarashina had not been Kanomata, who stood by Akutagawa's side; she'd been the girl with the short hair and cold eyes standing in the opposite corner—Konishi.

"The reason I picked on Kanomata was because she told terrible lies!" Sarashina shouted, her face twisting suddenly. "She cut up her own textbooks and her own notes. That's how she pretended she was getting bullied and how she elicited Kazushi's sympathy! I saw her cut up her notes, so I called her out and told her she was a liar. She was as silent as a stone when I did that. But she kept on deceiving Kazushi after that anyway, and he protected her as if she was a princess!

"But I'd always had a crush on Kazushi. And I saw him before she did! It wasn't fair...I couldn't talk to him, but she just kept getting closer and closer to him, and they were cuddling at the library every day, and—"

Sarashina's voice was growing louder and louder. Her hand shook as she gripped the chisel.

"She even persuaded Kazushi to buy her the rabbit doll I'd always wanted! 'Kazushi bought it for me,' she said and flashed it around on the field trip! I'd bought my rabbit with my allowance, but I threw it into the trash at the amusement park. I hated Kanomata so much my eyes burned. But the most unforgivable thing she did was snitch to Kazushi that I'd been bullying her!"

"She didn't do that! You've got it wrong, Sarashina," Akutagawa shouted. "I was the one who suspected you. And I was the one who told the teacher—it was all me!"

Akutagawa's admission only provoked Sarashina further.

"Are you protecting her?! Of course, she bad-mouthed me to

you! She *knew* that I liked you! But she was insufferable with her confidence that she was the one you liked. She would tell me, 'Kazushi is on my side' — I knew she was laughing at me in secret! That's why I picked on her! And I told everyone to be mean to her, too! I told them to say she was a lying temptress. Then she started acting weird, and during art class, she whispered 'I'm going to reveal the truth to Akutagawa.' Then she swung the chisel up and slashed me."

Sarashina laughed proudly. It looked to me like Sarashina was the one who was acting weird, and I shuddered. She laughed shrilly, her eyes bloodshot, then continued.

"That's why I did it! I grabbed my own chisel and turned it on Kanomata! I cut her arm, and once I'd jammed it in wherever I could, I stabbed her in the chest. I'll bet she still has the scar!"

I'd thought Konishi was the one who had been injured in the incident six years ago. Konishi — I mean, Sarashina had actually slashed Kanomata? But now I recalled what Akutagawa had said with pain in his voice. *"Kanomata's wounds haven't healed yet."* He also said that in his dreams, Kanomata had told him, "My wounds will last forever!"

Imagining the blood-soaked atrocity that had unfolded in that tiny classroom, I felt as if I was being swallowed up by heavy darkness.

Tohko's face was tense, too, and she seemed to be struggling to find something to say.

Sarashina just kept on talking.

About how her parents had never gotten along, and after the incident, they'd divorced after passing the blame for what their daughter had done back and forth to each other, and about how after Kanomata transferred, she had been forced to change schools, too.

How before she moved, Kanomata had come to see her and

151

apologized, leaving the language arts textbook and rabbit with her, saying "I want you to give these back to Akutagawa."

"What a Goody Two-shoes coming to apologize to the person she'd injured. Or maybe she was just exceptionally dim-witted."

Ice-cold rage showed in Sarashina's eyes.

"I cut off the rabbit's head with my chisel and cut 'Tangerines' out of the book. I was in the library once and heard her say, 'My favorite story in the textbook is Ryunosuke Akutagawa's story "Tangerines." I mean, his name is Akutagawa!' Ever since then, I'd hated that story. And then I cut out the 'Tangerines' pages and sent them and the rabbit to Kazushi's house under her name. I...couldn't throw out the rest of the book, so I kept it."

The last words alone she whispered with a touch of sadness.

Kanomata hadn't been the one to send the cut-out pages of "Tangerines" and the decapitated rabbit to Akutagawa. But it was still a bitter discovery for him.

It may actually have been better if they *had* been sent as a rejection from Kanomata.

Akutagawa knit his brows together deeply, tensed his jaw, and looked at Sarashina.

Her face had grown calm again. She gazed at Akutagawa and said, "I hate Goody Two-shoes like Kanomata who pretend to be so fragile...But I didn't mind becoming her if that was the kind of girl you liked.

"Kanomata was always, *always* interfering with you and me. In elementary school, she was stuck to you like glue and flaunted how close you two were. She's still taunting me. 'Akutagawa is on my side.' And 'This is payback for hurting me.' Even though it was her fault! She just won't go away! I can still feel what it felt like when I cut her. That's why I...became Kanomata. If I was her, there'd be no reason to fear her.

"And when I cut up books like she did, you came running,

didn't you, Kazushi? I was so happy. Every time I cut a book, you came. When I cut the rabbit, you ripped it out of my hands with a waxen face and told me, 'I'll take care of this somehow.' You were so worried about me, weren't you? You told Igarashi, 'She doesn't want to see you. Don't come near her again,' so I knew everything would be all right. There's nothing to interfere with us now, Kazushi. But we still can't be together? You're going to break up with me? Do I have to spend my birthday by myself next week?"

Akutagawa maintained his pained silence. I could tell he was conflicted, unable to cast off the girl he'd hurt to this extent. My breathing became strained. Tohko was looking at Akutagawa sadly.

Despair colored Sarashina's eyes.

"Maybe there's someone else you like? The girl who had this rabbit?" she murmured, putting one hand into a pocket, then thrusting a pink rabbit doll at Akutagawa.

Tohko gasped in surprise. My eyes widened, too.

Was that —?

"You didn't want to be in a play with me, but you'll be in one for the book club? Why? *Because Kotobuki is in it? She* is *beautiful and* so *popular with the boys.*"

So it *was* Kotobuki's rabbit! Sarashina had stolen it!

"Tell me! Do you like her?! Are you going out with her?! Did you give her this rabbit?!"

She set the rabbit down beside the bookshelf, then violently stabbed it with the chisel.

A gash yawned open on the rabbit's belly. She yanked the chisel to one side, cutting it apart.

"If so, I'll cut Nanase Kotobuki into ground beef!!!"

She howled, the chisel still plunged into the rabbit.

"I'll cut apart any girl—any one of them!—that you like, Kazushi!!!"

Akutagawa's shoulders were trembling. He bowed his head, then lifted it again immediately and shouted, "That's enough!! Just stop!"

Surprise showed on Sarashina's face.

Furrowing his brow and staring back at her, his breathing strained, Akutagawa continued with his biting words.

"I have no romantic feelings for you whatsoever. I can't keep covering for you anymore, and I'm not going to answer your summons."

Then he sucked in a short breath, his face looking tortured past its limits.

"Don't come near me again. I don't want to see you."

As he spoke, Sarashina's face transformed into something terribly sad. The rabbit dropped from the end of the chisel, and a tense silence filled the library.

"You finally...*gave me your answer.*"

Her voice was frail yet somehow relieved.

I was taken aback to see a sorrowful smile spread over her lips.

I'd seen a smile like that before.

It was the calm smile that had come over Miu's face on a summer day, on the windswept rooftop, her ponytail and the skirt of her uniform flying as she turned.

"Konoha, I don't think you would ever understand."

Miu falling.

Me screaming.

Something hot and sharp stabbing into my brain.

"No! Sarashina!"

I ran toward her. As I watched, she clutched the chisel in both hands and slashed it across her throat, a smile still on her face.

Time stopped.

Akutagawa was unable to move, his eyes wide; Tohko stood frozen, both hands over her mouth, and Takeda watched it all with a cool expression.

The fresh blood that spilled dyed Sarashina's body red.

She crumpled to the floor.

"Don't move her!" Tohko ordered as I bent over Sarashina. Takeda got her cell phone out of her pocket and called an ambulance. Tohko said, "I'll tell a teacher," and ran from the library.

"Sarashina...Sarashina!"

As I called to her, her eyes opened slightly and her blood-slick throat trembled. With much halting, she murmured, "You should have...told me...sooner...I'm not that bright...I didn't know..."

Sarashina seemed to whisper, *"I'm sorry."*

Shock coursed over Akutagawa's face as he stood frozen. He knelt down in the pool of blood, gripped his head in both hands, and he screamed.

"It's...it's always like this! It's always wrong! I swore I would never get it wrong again! I never wanted to hurt anyone this way again! If it was my fault you went crazy, I thought I had to take responsibility for it—but I was wrong—I drove you to this, Sarashina. I was wrong again! It's just like elementary school. I'm still a fool! Help her—help Sarashina...Help...please...Please help."

Akutagawa went on shouting, trembling. It was like I was seeing myself after Miu jumped off the roof.

"It's all right—everything's all right," I said.

My head was spinning, my throat burned, my mouth was dry, and I had trouble breathing. I couldn't have an attack now.

"It's all right. It'll be all right, Akutagawa."

I put an arm around his shoulders, which were far broader and

155

bulkier than my own, and repeated "it's all right" over and over, the only thing I knew how to say, while I had not the slightest faith that it really would be all right. I was shaking just like he was, but I simply prayed that Sarashina would be all right, that this nightmarish moment would pass quickly.

Takeda watched the two of us, wailing and trembling beside Sarashina, lying bloody on the floor, with an empty expression on her face.

<hr />

Help me, Mother. What should I do?

Your son has hurt someone again and thrown people's lives into disarray. Will I always be so foolish?

Sarashina fell to the floor, and her body was dyed red by the flow of her blood.

She gave me a pure smile and said, "You finally...*gave me your answer*," then slashed her throat. If I'd told her how I felt sooner, this wouldn't have happened. But no, even before that — if I'd refused when Igarashi asked me to bring her to the next archery match.

I wasn't sure what to do then, either. Could I be a matchmaker? Even though Sarashina was actually Konishi?!

In elementary school, I saddled her with a false accusation, cornered her, and drove her crazy.

I heard that her parents' divorce stemmed from that incident. It was as if I was the one who had broken Konishi's home.

When I started high school and ran into her again, I felt like my heart would stop. She didn't talk about what had happened, so I didn't either. But just being in the same room with her was torture. I felt like I was being punished.

So really, I wanted to refuse Igarashi's suggestion. But he

asked so many times I knew he was serious, and since I respected him as a person, I invited Sarashina to the match and introduced her to Igarashi. It was also a mistake to let her confide in me that he had been stalking her and to agree to act like I was her boyfriend. Igarashi quit the team because of that, and she slowly started to get crazier and crazier.

In the end, I was tied to my past crimes: I couldn't escape them, no matter how I struggled. I felt like I still needed to atone for what I'd done, as if Konishi and Kanomata still hadn't forgiven me for the mistakes I'd made in the past.

I was desperate. I worked hard to make amends for my crime, to be smarter so I wouldn't make a mistake this time. But it didn't work. The actions I took, the path I chose, all of it, everything — it was all wrong.

How can I apologize to Kanomata, to Konishi, to Ms. Momoki, to Igarashi, to Sarashina?

I'm just going in circles in a dark, impenetrable maze. My ears are roaring, my body feels like it's burning, and my head feels like it's going to split. I can't even stand up straight.

Mother, if you can't help me, at least judge me. I want you to decide for me. Even if your judgment is death, I will obey.

Please, Mother: Answer me. Mother! Mother!

Chapter 6 – A Fool's Labyrinth

An ambulance took Sarashina to a nearby hospital where she was treated. That was three days ago.

If the cut had been just a little farther to one side, it would have all been over for her, but she was treated quickly enough. The cut wasn't as deep as it had looked, so she wasn't in any danger, and they said she would be able to go home in a week. Maki was the one who came to tell us all this.

That day, Tohko had gone with Sarashina to the hospital. The rest of us went to the principal's office to explain what had happened; then we waited on a sofa for news from the hospital.

That was when Maki appeared and told us, "Tohko called me. The girl's all right.

"And there was that bloodshed just the other day, too. Unbelievable. How can so many problems be cropping up at a *school*? It's not easy to hush things up so they don't reach the students. Still, I'm sure my grandfather will handle it just fine. You can all go home now. I doubt you're in the mood to go to classes or your clubs. I'll have you driven home." Looking over at Akutagawa, she said, "That boy there in particular seems like he wouldn't make it home. How would it look if he threw himself off a bridge on the way home?"

I didn't think that was very funny.

But that was how worn out and ragged Akutagawa was. After a temporary descent into madness, he had become as mute as a stone and only barely responded to even the teachers' questions. His twisted face and strained breathing told me that he still blamed himself, and I worried about what he would do to the point that anxiety squeezed my chest. If the worst had happened to Sarashina, it would have destroyed his mind.

That night I got a phone call from Tohko. Sarashina had mostly calmed down, and Tohko had been able to talk with her a little.

But even hearing that didn't cheer me up.

Three days passed after that, and the culture fair was closing in next week.

Rehearsals for the play had been on hiatus the whole time. Tohko and Takeda had been busy helping out with preparations for their classes' events. I'd seen Tohko yesterday, scampering down the hall, her hair in weird, uneven braids.

Kotobuki wanted to know why Akutagawa and I had left class during lunch and then gone home early three days before, but I only told her that I hadn't felt well and didn't talk about what happened.

"Then I'll ask Akutagawa," she had said in a huff. But shock broke over her face when she saw how wasted Akutagawa looked when he came to school, and she hadn't said a word about it since.

Though I doubted that he spared even a moment for comfort during his self-recrimination, Akutagawa dutifully attended classes, never missing school and always on time.

When Miu jumped off the roof, I'd shut myself up in my room. But it looked like Akutagawa had shut himself up in a room inside his heart.

If I talked to him, he would answer, but he always looked pained, as if he was thinking about something else.

Tohko came to our class during lunch.

"I was thinking we need to start rehearsals back up again soon. How do you feel about that?" she asked Akutagawa gently, considerate of his feelings.

"All right. I'll be at the auditorium after school today," he answered indifferently.

For the first time in ages, we began dress rehearsals, but the mood was strange.

Everyone was thinking about Akutagawa, wondering if he was all right, and our voices had a tendency to fall into monotone.

Akutagawa went through Omiya's lines with a dark expression on his face. There was none of the tension that had been in his voice before, and he had almost no inflection when he spoke. But he continued to recite the lines, as if he was carrying out a duty he had been charged with.

During the climactic exchange of letters between Omiya and Sugiko, Akutagawa suddenly broke off in his dialogue.

In the scene, Omiya has gone abroad, and Sugiko has been sending him letters confessing her passion and begging, "Please accept me." Omiya has always responded, "Please, love Nojima, not me," but he inadvertently reveals his true feelings and accepts her.

"I wondered whether to send this letter or if I had better not. I think it would be better not to. However —"

No matter how many times Akutagawa and Kotobuki did it, it was the same. Like a broken CD, as soon as he reached that line, his voice broke off.

It happened again the next day and the day after that. It was too painful to see him struggle to force the line out, his brow deeply knit and his eyes narrowed. I couldn't watch.

So it went, until the last day before the culture fair.

When I got to the auditorium, Kotobuki was onstage, practicing her lines by herself.

"Please don't be angry, Mister Omiya. It took all of my courage to write to you."

She faced the audience with an intent gaze and pleaded ardently. She looked remarkably vulnerable, nothing like her usual self.

"I await your reply, but still it has not come. I begin to worry. Are you angry, I wonder? Please have pity on me and write back."

She jumped when she noticed me and blushed.

"G-geez. Why didn't you say something when you came in?"

"Sorry. You were just so wrapped up in your rehearsal. Where's everyone else?"

Kotobuki looked away and muttered an answer. "I guess they're busy with their classes…The performance is tomorrow, though. Will Akutagawa be all right?"

Her face looked suddenly timid again as her eyes darted back to me.

My face gloomy, I answered, "He said he would go on, but…"

I knew why he stopped during that line. He could see his love triangle with Igarashi and Sarashina in Omiya's situation, and even if it was only a play, Akutagawa was afraid to betray his best friend Nojima and accept Sugiko, the woman Nojima loved. It frightened him because by betraying Igarashi and listening to Sarashina's plea, he had driven both Igarashi and Sarashina into a corner.

161

Was this the right choice? Wasn't this wrong? That anxiety made him stumble over the line.

Should we be forcing Akutagawa to go onstage in that case? I wondered. If he froze up during the show, wouldn't that just add to the indelible wounds he already had?

Kotobuki was probably worried, too. She looked away and hung her head.

I set my bag down in a seat without a word.

"…Hey," Kotobuki murmured, still turned away. "Practice with me until everyone gets here. Can you read Omiya's lines for me? I want to get a feel for the last scene."

I nodded and climbed onto the stage.

"Okay. Let's start from the part where they're exchanging letters," I said.

"…Right. What about your script?"

"I've pretty much got it memorized."

"…Oh."

We stood at either end of the stage.

Kotobuki gazed at me with vulnerable, dewy eyes.

"Please don't be angry, Mister Omiya. It took all of my courage to write you."

Was she acting? Her voice was trembling slightly.

The slight upward turn of her eyes, the way she held her hands clasped in front of her, she was the exact image of an innocent young girl summoning all her courage to tell the person she liked how she felt. I felt strange.

For some reason, my heart started pounding.

Was it beating faster because of Kotobuki?

It couldn't have been that, but an anxious, tender feeling welled up inside me.

"I await your reply, but still it has not come. I begin to worry. Are you angry, I wonder? Please have pity on me and write back."

162

It wasn't only Kotobuki's voice that was trembling. Her laced fingers, her lips, her eyelashes — all wavered faintly.

"I am yours, sir. I am yours."

Kotobuki looked straight at me, her face rapt.

"My life, my honor, my happiness, my pride — all are yours, sir. All are yours."

Her voice became more and more charged with emotion, tinged with excitement, and tears pooled in the corners of her eyes.

"By becoming yours, I will for the first time become myself."

For some reason, at that moment, I recalled the day Kotobuki and I had talked alone at the hospital.

"You may not remember it, but I ... in middle school, I ..."

Had she looked like this then? Been this close to tears?

Suddenly, she hung her head and stopped reciting her lines.

I was just wondering what had happened when a clear bead slid down Kotobuki's cheek.

Was — was she actually crying?!

"Wh-what's wrong, Kotobuki?"

I hurried over to her.

"Did you just get too into the part? Or are you still worried about Akutagawa and —"

"No!" Kotobuki sobbed, shaking her head. "It's not because I'm worried about Akutagawa. I'm an awful person. Akutagawa's in pain, and everyone's so worried about him, but ... I'm so wrapped up in something else it's driving me crazy."

She covered her face with her hands, her shoulders shaking.

I was at a loss. I didn't know what to do.

"What's bothering you so much?"

Kotobuki gave several childish sobs. Then, her hands still covering her face, she said in a feeble voice, "Y-you ... You're always late or leaving early or ducking out at lunch ... or whispering with Tohko and Takeda ... I, I figured it was ... something about

Akutagawa, that you guys don't want other people to know. I can tell that much at least. I...I'm not usually like this...I hate being so spineless, and usually I'm not. B-but...I think Takeda knows... But you hate me. You won't be open with me."

My heart clenched intensely.

She must have been upset because she felt like she was being left out. She may have put on a brave face, but inside she had been hurt.

"I'm sorry I didn't see how you felt. But I don't hate you, you know."

"You...you jerk." Kotobuki choked up tearfully, looking up again. "Jerk! You're unbelievable! Just...you jerk..."

She railed at me, her face a total mess. I couldn't tell if she was being aggressive or weak, if she was angry or crying.

"I'm not really sure why, but...I'm sorry."

"If you don't know why you're apologizing, then don't do it! I hate that about you. You're nice to everyone and pleasant and polite, and it infuriates me...It makes me sad. In middle school, it was — you weren't like that. You used to smile because you were actually happy."

That surprised me.

"You knew me in middle school? You mentioned something about that in the hospital, too."

Kotobuki looked at me, taken aback. Her expression was as unguarded as a child's, and it worked its way into my heart and halted its beating.

The auditorium fell into utter silence.

"I —," she began in a frail voice. Her cheeks were colored bright red. "I met you once in middle school."

"I'm sorry, where was that?"

Kotobuki bit down on her lip a little and lowered her eyes.

"I'm sure you don't remember. But it meant a lot to me. So I went to see you again after that. Over and over, all through the winter. Every day."

I couldn't fathom it. Every single day? Where was she? Why didn't I remember meeting her?

"You always looked like you were enjoying yourself back then. You were always happy and smiling. That girl was always at your side."

I felt as if I'd suddenly been slashed across the face. Kotobuki lifted her gaze once again.

"You were always, always with that girl. She was the only thing you ever looked at, and you would laugh so happily. But when I met you in high school, you didn't enjoy yourself at all, didn't talk to anyone honestly. But you still had a bright smile on the outside and pretended to be having fun. I hated it...I mean, I finally got to meet you, but you weren't the same person."

Oh no — I was having trouble breathing.

Her words became frigid chains, coiling layer over layer around my throat. My pulse raced, and my fingertips started to get numb. My mind reeled.

It was happening again.

Oh no, oh no.

Kotobuki's face crumpled, and she looked even closer to tears than before.

"When Igarashi got stabbed behind the school, and I heard Sarashina screaming 'It's that girl's fault!' it was like I was seeing myself, and I shuddered. In my heart, I felt like it was that girl's fault that you'd changed, and I resented her. Like because of her — because of Miu Inoue, you stopped laughing! It's true, isn't it? That girl — *the girl who was always with you was the author Miu Inoue, wasn't she!*"

The chains coiled around my neck tightened — *snap!* — against my throat. I felt the pain of them biting into my skin as my mind went white, and all sound was sucked out of the world.

Why was she talking about Miu?!

Kotobuki finally seemed to notice the odd change occurring in my body.

"I-Inoue...?"

I had trouble breathing and could barely stand. My vision clouded over, and I fell to my knees on the stage. At that very moment—

"Sorry I'm late."

"Hello Konoha, hello Nanase."

Akutagawa came into the auditorium with Takeda close behind him.

"I ran into Akutagawa right outside so we came together. Heh-heh. Oh—Konoha, are you sweating? You look terrible."

I pressed hard against my chest, took a deep breath, and answered, "...It was so hot in here. I'm fine now."

The pulse I felt beneath the palm of my hand was still racing, but sound had come back to the world and somehow I managed to stand up. My brain ached as if I had been punched in the head, and if I wasn't careful, I felt sure I would have another attack.

Kotobuki must have regretted unleashing her feelings on me, because she bit down on her lip and was trying not to look at me.

"Sorry everybody! The prep work for my class's curry restaurant ran late."

Tohko ran in, her long braids fluttering.

With everyone present, our final rehearsal began.

"What a lovely voice."

"It's her. I know it."

"How fortunate for you if that's true."

167

Nojima and Omiya continued their dialogue.

I couldn't get what Kotobuki had said to me out of my head.

"...I felt like it was that girl's fault that you'd changed, and I resented her.

"...It's true, isn't it? That girl — the girl who was always with you was the author Miu Inoue, wasn't she!"

I didn't know why Kotobuki had mistaken Miu for Miu Inoue. But she definitely knew about the two of us.

She knew about how I had been happy and enjoyed myself just having Miu around, how I had been idiotically cheerful, how I had always looked at Miu so affectionately.

If I revisited my memories of middle school, Miu was always there.

In the classroom in the morning, in the hall during breaks, on the road home in the sunset, at the convenience store we went to all the time on the way home, getting food from street vendors, at the park where falling ginkgo leaves filled the air, at the old library, at the pastry shop she forced me to go to with her — no matter the scene, Miu was there. Looking at me, her hair up in a ponytail, then smiling teasingly.

"You're special to me, Konoha. So I'm going to tell you what my dream is.

"I'm gonna be a writer. Tons of people are going to read my books. It would be awesome if that made them happy.

"The book I'm writing now is almost done. You're gonna be the first to read it.

"Hee-hee. You're blushing, Konoha. What's wrong? What are you thinking about? Fess up. I promise I won't get mad. Okay? Tell me what you're thinking. All of it. Tell me every. last. thing. about you, Konoha."

But then one day, all of a sudden, Miu looked at me with daggers.

She ignored me and avoided me, and with a final smile, she said, "You wouldn't understand," then jumped off the roof right in front of me.

The smile Sarashina had given before she slashed her throat in the library mingled with how Miu had looked then, and it had swelled to fill my brain.

"You finally . . . gave me your answer."

Fresh blood seeping out of her.

Akutagawa gaping at her in shock.

"You should have . . . told me . . . sooner . . . I'm not that bright . . . I didn't know . . .

". . . I'm sorry."

My chest constricted, and my throat burned.

I tried to make it go away, but the image wouldn't fade. I saw Miu's face, Sarashina's face, Akutagawa's face. They all looked sad and disappointed.

Where had we gone wrong?

Akutagawa hadn't meant to hurt Sarashina; all he'd wanted was to make up for his past mistakes. And all Sarashina had done was care for Akutagawa that whole time.

So why had it gone wrong?

Had I also hurt Miu without realizing it? Had I made a mistake somehow, somewhere?

Was that why Miu started to hate me and why she'd jumped off the roof?

"When you asked me to come watch a match, I was so happy.

"...Whenever you invited me somewhere, I dressed up super-nice and would go to the place we were supposed to meet ten minutes early, my heart pounding the whole time."

Akutagawa had always believed that he needed to be smart, he needed to be honorable. He chose his actions torn between the upperclassman he respected and the girl he had wounded in the past.

When he realized that those actions had only invited more unhappiness, the pain and despair he felt had pierced my heart, as well.

Onstage, Akutagawa and Kotobuki were rehearsing the climactic correspondence scene between Omiya and Sugiko. I watched them from the wings, my heart wrenching.

"Please, Mister Omiya, I want you to see me as an independent human being, as a woman."

"Please don't batter my plea with the stones you call friendship."

Akutagawa looked pained. His face twisted, and he gritted his teeth, sweat beading up on his forehead.

If he opened his mouth and accepted her, something would change fundamentally.

And there was no guarantee that his excruciating decision would be the right one.

"...It's always like this! It's always wrong! I swore I would never get it wrong again!...

"I was wrong again! It's just like elementary school. I'm still a fool! Help her—help Sarashina."

Akutagawa's pain blended into Omiya's conflict, and my own suffering blended into that.
Why did we hurt people?
Why did we break things?

"... Why did you say we should break up, Kazushi?"

"I don't think you would ever understand, Konoha."

"I tried my best. I always loved you, Kazushi."

"I don't think you would ever understand, Konoha."

"I wondered whether to send this letter or if I had better not. I think it would be better not to. However—"
He stopped.
Sweat trickled down Akutagawa's cheek. His dry lips merely trembled; no words emerged. He stood there, unable to move.
Why did he have to keep performing when it was so difficult for him?
Why did he have to make such a firm commitment when it sliced him apart?
What if his decision was the wrong one?
If he hurt someone again?
If something broke again?
My throat twinged shut, and I broke out in a cold sweat. I was helpless in the face of a pain that threatened to rip my body in two, and I balled my fists up and screamed, "Just stop already!

Haven't you done enough? Why do you have to suffer like this?!"

Akutagawa and Kotobuki looked at me in surprise, as did Tohko and Takeda, who stood in the wings on the other side of the stage.

The auditorium fell quiet, and the air felt painfully tense. I trembled as I spoke.

"It's just a culture fair. I was never into it in the first place. Just forget about it. I'm not going on tomorrow."

I felt a searing pain in my head, and a hot lump rose in my throat. I got down from the stage, picked up my bag from the seat it was on, and walked toward the door.

"Konoha, what's the matter? You're *really* not going on tomorrow?"

Takeda ran up and pulled me back.

I gently shook her hand from my arm and said, my head still bowed, "I'm sorry."

Then I left the auditorium like a fugitive.

I got home and crawled into bed, breathing shallowly through my twitching throat. My fingertips were numb, and I let out a rasping sound like a broken flute from the back of my throat. I felt a splitting pain in my head, as if it was being pressed on either side by iron walls.

Why was I so weak and pathetic and stupid?

Whenever anything happened, my body stopped working right, and I let loose these childish tantrums and then ran away.

What must they all think? Especially Tohko...

It hurt. I couldn't breathe. It was awful. I was awful. An awful, world-class idiot.

How long would it take for me to be okay again? Would I be like this my whole life?

Miu!
Miu!
Miu!
Why can't I ever forget about you?
Behind my tightly closed eyes, I pictured Nojima's, Omiya's, and Sugiko's lines, one after another. Bloodred words cascaded down around me as I huddled in an endless expanse of darkness, bound by chains.

"They say those who have truly loved will never be brokenhearted."

"That seems so sad, almost unbearably sad."

"When I dream of that girl, I feel so desolate I hardly know what to do, and I think, I truly will never be brokenhearted."

"I will refrain. I will do what I can. But please grant me one small thing."

"I beg you. Let me have Sugiko. Don't take her from me."

"I pray for your happiness."

"I can't bear to be at Mister Nojima's side more than an hour."

"I cannot steal the woman my best friend loves."

"I will never be Mister Nojima's wife. I would rather die."

Many letters.
Many words.

Painful words.

Bitter words.

Heartrending words.

"I don't think you would ever understand, Konoha."

I shouldn't have fallen in love with you.

I shouldn't have ever met you.

Then I never would have had to experience the pain, the fear, the sadness of being cast down alone into this darkness.

I didn't want to be close to anyone ever again.

I didn't want to feel this way.

My little sister Maika came to tell me dinner was ready.

"Are you sick, Konoha?"

My tiny sister looked at me tearfully. "Tell Mom I already ate," I answered, then pulled the covers over my head and huddled in my bed.

I knew I was making my family worry again.

I was disgusted by my childishness and I hated it, but I couldn't help that it felt like my head was going to split open and I could barely breathe.

I must have been lying there for almost four hours.

When I finally got my breathing under control, my room was dark and it was raining outside.

I listened to the cold sound of the rain.

I rolled my head to look over at the window and saw that the part slick with rain was glistening faintly.

I dragged myself out of bed and walked over to the window to close the curtain. I glanced outside, where the light spilling from the porch light and windows of the houses next door faintly illuminated the road and buildings.

A single red flower stood out in bloom in the midst of the light.

Someone was standing at a bend in the road, looking up at my house.

A girl who was holding a red umbrella and wearing the uniform of my school.

"...Kotobuki?"

Startled, I left my room. Treading quietly down the stairs so my family wouldn't hear me, I opened the front door and went outside.

When she saw me, Kotobuki's shoulders jumped; then she gripped the handle of her umbrella tightly in both hands and looked down timidly.

"...I'm sorry."

Her faint, broken voice was almost lost in the sound of the falling rain.

"It's...my fault you got angry and left, right? 'Cos I mentioned that girl...I'm sorry. I don't know what I should do..."

"...It's not your fault, Kotobuki."

My voice was hoarse. I was exhausted and had no strength left in my body, so I had no energy to spare for kind words.

"But—"

Kotobuki shrunk in on herself.

"Really, it...has nothing to do with you. So could you just leave?"

Kotobuki looked up at me, her eyes terribly sad. She looked wounded, which made my heart ache.

"I'm sorry," she whispered faintly, then hurried off. I saw that the shoulders and back of her uniform were darker where the cloth had been thoroughly soaked, and I realized she must have been standing in the rain for a very long time.

My chest tightened, and I was having trouble breathing

again — but I refused to think about it anymore and went back to my house.

I softly opened the front door, and as I was going upstairs, my mother came out of the living room.

"How do you feel, Konoha?" she asked worriedly.

"I'm fine, Mom."

"I still have your dinner ready. And the bath is warmed up."

I was about to tell her I wasn't hungry when I remembered Kotobuki's sad eyes. My heart constricting, I pressed my lips together and said, "Thanks. I'll eat after my bath."

My late dinner seemed to stick in my throat, and I could barely taste it. But nevertheless, I ate every scrap of it and washed the dishes in the kitchen before going back to my room.

Even after I turned the lights out and lay in bed, I listened to the sound of the cold rain, totally unable to fall asleep.

I didn't want to hurt anyone or to be hurt anymore, but it kept happening...and the wounds I caused would be revisited on me.

Maybe it wasn't possible for people to live without hurting others. Maybe as a species, we're just that stupid.

I'd said awful things to Kotobuki.

And how was I going to face Akutagawa and Takeda and Tohko?

What was going to happen to the play at the fair?

Speaking of which...Tohko hadn't called me. With that thought, my consciousness slipped away into a muddy darkness.

<hr />

Sarashina was released from the hospital.

Mother — I couldn't go to see her even once.

I couldn't decide if it was right to go see her or right not to go see her or if I should apologize or if I should ignore what happened.

I hurt her. Not just physically, but emotionally — I've hurt her so many times since that day six years ago. But I meant to be an honorable person.

Mother — I don't even know what the word *honor* means anymore. What is it? What does it take to be honorable? Doesn't being honorable on the one hand mean being dishonorable on the other?

I don't know. I don't know what's right or what I ought to do. Or who I ought to choose.

I received another letter from her today. I still can't make myself read it.

Why did I think that someone like me might be able to help her? Why did I think something so arrogant even briefly?

Mother, I am a fool.

P.S.
The play looks like it's on hold. I'm sure that I've hurt Inoue, too.

Chapter 7 – The Book Girl's Wish

When I woke up, my head felt leaden.

I glanced over at the clock beside my bed.

I should get up soon...

But I didn't want to go to school. I didn't want to be in the play.

I wanted to snivel and shut myself away like I had in middle school. But when I thought about how sad my family would be, I crawled out of bed in resignation.

"Good morning, Konoha. Do you want some breakfast?"

"...Okay."

I ate the bacon and eggs, the toast smeared with apple jelly, the corn soup, and the vegetable juice without really tasting any of it, just like dinner the night before.

"See you tonight."

I slung my bag over my shoulder and went out the door.

Maybe I would go somewhere else now. To the movies or an Internet café...

I set out onto the road, thinking it over, when —

"Good morning, Konoha."

*   *   *

The rain had stopped, the air was cool, and bright light shone down from a clear sky.

The faint scent of rain still lingered on the street, where Tohko stood holding a poetry collection by Robert Browning. She looked at me, then smiled brilliantly.

"I came to get you. Let's walk together."

It was the same look she'd had when, just after I started high school and she forced me to join the book club, she would come to my classroom every day to get me, so I didn't skip out and go home.

A kind, radiant look.

"All right, Konoha, it's time for a club meeting."

Tohko closed the poetry collection, then moved to stand in front of me with a little bounce. Her long braids like cats' tails bounded in the air together.

Tohko cocked her head like she always did, as if nothing was the matter, and looked up at me brightly, which made my throat burn and my chest swell.

"...You're such a busybody," I said, choking back the feelings rising up in me, my voice trembling. "You always, always have to stick your nose in. I'm tired of it. I don't want to be in the play. Akutagawa will be better off, too."

I was like a child throwing a tantrum, and Tohko was like a mother as she asked, her face kind, "Is the reason you don't want to be in the play because it's so hard to watch Akutagawa suffering? Or is it because you're in pain yourself?"

"Both."

Tohko's face drooped a little.

"Oh... but if you do that, you and Akutagawa will just keep on suffering."

179

"I'm fine with that. It's better than going out of your way for something, then failing and suffering even more."

Tohko drooped even more.

Her sad, concerned face always worked on me.

"After you went home yesterday, Akutagawa didn't say anything, but he looked agonized. Don't you think Akutagawa needs our help right now?"

"I can't. I can barely look after myself."

I trembled, bowing my head. Tohko's glum but clear voice was like fresh water when she spoke.

"You know...when you started second year and I saw you talking to Akutagawa in your classroom, I was so happy for you. I thought, 'Oh good, Konoha's made a friend.' Ever since your first year, you'd never tried to make friends with anyone, and it seemed like you always kept a distance between you and other people when you talked to them.

"I always thought it would be nice if you made friends.

"I mean, I'm going to be gone next year after I graduate. Then you're going to be the only one in the book club."

Was she saying that the reason she'd been so fired up to secure members was not to preserve the book club, but because she was worried about leaving me on my own?

And the reason she'd been so elated about Akutagawa being in the play and the reason she never stepped aside in the club was because she didn't want to leave me on my own...?

I was afraid the kindness in Tohko's voice might make me cry, and I quickly blinked the tears away.

"You are such an unbelievable nuisance. You always jerk me around and say the most selfish things...I've never wanted any friends, and I never felt like getting to know anybody. Relationships that go on forever only exist in naive stories, and if you do believe in them, then when you get betrayed, all you get is pain.

"If a relationship is just going to fall apart some day, it's better not to get involved at all.

"And then there's Akutagawa...I wanted to stay in the comfortable relationship we had before. But you had to butt in and force him to be in the play and investigate everything he's ever done—you forced me to find out all this stuff about him that I didn't want to know!"

And now I was just as bad as Ms. Momoki when she shifted the blame onto Akutagawa. If I said anything more, I would hurt Tohko. I was tired of these uncontrollable, childish emotions. I was tired of all of it.

"I didn't want to know any of it...I didn't want to be close to anyone...I wish I'd never met any of them..."

I wish I'd never met Miu or Akutagawa, either.

Tohko's face fell, and she looked at me sadly.

Don't say another word, Konoha.

I pressed my lips together and hung my head.

"So you think you would have been better off if you'd never met me?"

When I lifted my face, Tohko's clear, black eyes were fixed straight, unavoidably, on me.

"...Grah."

My heart was pierced, my eyelids burned, and my throat convulsed.

"...That's not fair."

Yeah. It wasn't fair.

It was a totally unfair, cowardly question.

The many smiles, the kindnesses, the advice Tohko had given me up till now flashed through my mind one after another, and something hot welled up deep in my chest.

At the end of a long winter—under a snow-white magnolia tree on the school grounds—I met Tohko.

"I am Tohko Amano, in class eight of the second-years. As you can see, I am a book girl."

"All right, Konoha, today's prompts are 'watermelon,' 'the bullet train,' and 'a gas tank.' You have precisely fifty minutes. Write an extra-sweet story! And...GO!"

"Waaah, this story is way too spicy, Konoha!"

"I am not a goblin! I'm just a book girl!"

She was an audacious, happy-go-lucky, and unorthodox club president who munched on paper; she jerked people around mercilessly; she had me hard at work writing her snacks; she forced me to write improv stories every single solitary day, even though I never wanted to write another novel ever again; and she said they were bitter or sour or whatever, then gobbled them all down without leaving a scrap behind —

She acted selfishly, but sometimes she would seem concerned. She would say warm, kind things to me.

Tohko was the only one that I couldn't lie to, just as Akutagawa found it impossible to lie to his mother.

After all, Tohko had seen me be weak and pathetic this whole time.

She knew all about my cowardice and my stupidity.

And so she was the only person I couldn't lie to.

And then to ask me if I wished I had never met her — it wasn't fair asking me that.

She already knew the answer.

No fair! No fair at all!

How totally unfair of you, Tohko!

"Gah…that's not a fair question. It's not fair to ask me that when you already know…"

The tears I'd been holding back welled up in my eyes, but I kept arguing "it's not fair" through my sobs. Tohko walked up to me and reached out her white hands to cup my cheeks. It was a cool, gentle sensation.

My nerves relaxed, but I kept my face down as more tears spilled from my eyes. Tohko whispered a line from the play in her clear, kind voice.

"I believe in you. You will be victorious. Your goodness and sincerity will help you grow to great things. I will be with you when you feel all alone. Walk the path you believe in with commitment. Your path will be long, and fools will disparage you. But you have a destiny that only you can fulfill."

My voice thick with emotion, I answered, "That's…not something Sugiko actually said. It's just one of Nojima's fantasies."

"That's true. But I'm not a fantasy."

The hands that had cupped my cheeks moved to hold my hands. Then she pressed my hands over her heart.

"I'm really here."

Her intelligent eyes looked straight into mine.

Below the jacket and shirt of her uniform, I felt Tohko's heartbeat. It carried all the way into my palm.

Tohko's chest was bony and hard, but it was warm, and beneath her skin, I could feel the proof that Tohko was alive and that she existed.

*Thump…thump…*it went.

I couldn't stop crying.

My throat and my chest felt like they were ripping apart, and my hot tears gushed out of me like water from a broken faucet.

As I listened to the sound of Tohko's heartbeat with my hand, I realized something.

I had decided that after Miu, I would never get attached to anyone ever again. But I realized that all this time, I had been growing deeply attached to Tohko.

That after crying pitifully like this in front of her and spewing my feelings at her, each time I had felt the warmth of Tohko's hands, and I had gotten back up.

I couldn't possibly wish that I'd never met Tohko.

"Now, now, stop crying. You can use my handkerchief."

Gently slipping her hand out from our overlapped grip, Tohko pulled out a light blue handkerchief. I accepted it, and pressing it against my face, I said, "This is the handkerchief I lent you."

"What?!"

"That was more than three months ago."

"O-oh? Was it really?" Tohko mumbled. Then she went on in embarrassment, "After you wipe your face, shall we go to school?"

"Yeah."

After I'd splashed some water on my face at the sink at school, I headed to my class.

In the space of a day, the classroom had been transformed into a manga café. The desks were pushed together to make tables, which we set around the room with chairs; the manga everyone had brought from home were lined up on shelves; and billboards with anime characters on them had been hung up.

"Is Akutagawa here yet?" I asked. A classmate told me, "He's doing some morning practice at the archery hall."

I went to the practice hall and found Akutagawa all alone in his archery uniform and facing a target.

He drew back on the bow in his hand; straightened his spine; stared at the target with a tense, firm expression; and then released the arrow.

The arrow skirted the target and lodged into the matting propped up behind it. When he saw that, his brow furrowed in pain.

"Akutagawa?"

I called out to him, and his eyes widened in surprise.

"Inoue —"

"Sorry about yesterday. Something's been getting to me, too, lately, and I just boiled over. I was trying to run away. But I stopped running. So I was wondering if you would be in the play with me. We could confront the things we're afraid of there."

Akutagawa's eyes grew even wider, and he looked down at me.

I lifted my face up to look back at him.

Without fear, smiling, dignified.

The surprise in Akutagawa's eyes gradually shifted into an optimistic determination.

"All right."

He nodded, then smiled just a little.

In that moment, I felt as if a refreshing feeling of empathy had flowed into my lungs along with the pure morning air.

When I returned to the classroom with Akutagawa, who had now changed back into his uniform, it was oddly abuzz.

Had there been some kind of crisis?

Just then, Kotobuki's friend Mori ran up to me.

"It's terrible, Inoue! Nanase collapsed, and they took her to the nurse's office! They said it was a cold. She was burning up!"

"She what?!"

Akutagawa and I both ran down to the nurse's office and found Kotobuki lying on a bed breathing raggedly, her face bright red.

"I...I'm sorry, Inoue. I—"

She looked at me, tears in her eyes.

"I'll still be in the play," she croaked. Something about her admirable display of intensity lodged in my heart.

"You can't. You should call your family and go home."

"But then I'll be causing everyone so much trouble."

"You couldn't help it, Kotobuki. It's my fault you got sick."

The reason she had become sick was because she'd stood out in the rain for such a long time. I couldn't let her feel like she was responsible.

"It's okay. We'll take care of the play."

I said this with a smile empty of all falsehood, and Kotobuki's eyes teared up again.

"O-okay..."

"Whaaaat? Nanase collapsed with a fever?!" Tohko shouted, her eyes bugging out. She was dressed as a maid, acting as waitress in her class's curry restaurant.

"Would you play Sugiko for her, Tohko? I bet you have all the lines memorized anyway," I said.

"What about Nojima?"

"I'll do it," I answered crisply. Tohko's eyes widened slightly; then she quickly smiled and nodded.

"All right."

Akutagawa then asked, "If you play Nojima, then who'll play Hayakawa?"

"Hayakawa hardly has any lines, so we can cut him out with some ad-libbing."

"That's true. Let's do that. There's hardly any time left before the curtain goes up. We have to get Chia and discuss everything."

At that moment, Maki appeared with a sketchbook in her arms.

"Bonjour, Tohko! I came to behold your maid costume. I see that a true beauty really can look good in anything."

"Argh! Why are you here?! My manager told you I wouldn't be here till this afternoon!"

"You didn't expect such an obvious lie to deceive me, did you? Now surrender yourself and let me sketch you."

Tohko pulled off her apron and shoved it at Maki.

"Unfortunately something extremely urgent has come up. I've gotta go."

"Hey, Tohko! Your shift's not up yet!"

One of her classmates, also dressed as a maid, rushed over to stop her. Tohko pointed at Maki.

"Make her do it instead."

"Wait, *what*? Tohkoooo!"

Takeda was dressed in a short festival jacket, selling octopus dumplings from a stall in the school yard, when we met up with her. By the time we'd talked about the changes in the performance, changed into costume, and run into the auditorium, it was only five minutes before the curtain went up.

I stood in the wings with Takeda, our chests heaving as we got our breathing under control.

I was sure that Tohko and Akutagawa were standing by on the opposite side in a similar state.

"That...was pretty close," said Takeda.

"Y-yeah."

"I'm glad you came today and didn't blow the play off. You *are* the one who told me I had to live."

I glanced over and saw that Takeda wasn't smiling. Her face and the whisper of her voice were both quite soft and detached.

"I'm just like you, Takeda. I've been wearing a mask this whole time and avoided getting close to people. But if I see this play through to the end, I think I might be able to get past that part of myself. And not just me — Akutagawa might, too."

"I'd like to see that. If it works, I'll have some hope, too."

The stage was as dark as a night that goes on into eternity. I couldn't make anything out on the other side.

I wondered what Akutagawa was thinking about right now.

I wanted to overcome this together.

I prayed for it so powerfully my heart trembled.

Please, please.

A buzzer rang to announce the curtain's rising, and we stepped out onto the stage.

In spotlights like moonbeams, Akutagawa and I proceeded slowly past the unopened curtain, he from stage right and I from stage left.

"This is the story of myself, my truest friend Omiya, and the woman I loved."

My voice went out quietly into the auditorium through the microphone fixed to my collar.

Then came Akutagawa's deep, resolute voice.

"This is the story of myself, my truest friend Nojima, and the woman he loved."

The curtain silently lifted, and a third spotlight lit up the center of the stage, illuminating Tohko's slender back.

Her straight black hair reached her hips. A big ribbon was tied at the back of her head. She wore a bewitching pink kimono with fluttering sleeves and burgundy empire-waisted pants.

"I first met Sugiko in the hallway outside the second floor of the Imperial Theater."

I wasn't a professional actor, so of course my performance wasn't spectacular. I merely pictured the person Nojima was in my mind, overlaid his emotions on my own, and worked hard to say his lines in a loud, clear voice.

For now, Akutagawa's voice was steady, too.

When Tohko turned and sent her hair fluttering, the packed seats of the audience were filled with gasps of appreciation.

That was how pretty, how beautiful without hyperbole Tohko looked with her hair down, her entire bearing redolent of a book girl from an older, purer age. She was like a violet blossom announcing the advent of spring.

"Where are you going?"

"To my flower lessons."

The always-pumped hyperactivity she had when she played Nojima was ratcheted down to a nice level in her performance as Sugiko. The way she recited her lines and her movements as she dipped her head at Nojima were both simple and pretty.

I watched Sugiko walk away gracefully the way Nojima would have, thinking, *Ah, this is the most beautiful flower nature has made.*

A being that is gentle, noble, dreamlike.

"Precious, precious girl. I will be a man worthy of becoming your husband. Until I am, I beg you not to marry another."

I knew what it felt like to pray so hard for something.

To be happy just looking at the person you love for your heart to leap, to tirelessly imagine things turning out well for yourself, and to love a person ceaselessly to the point of foolishness.

My feelings for Miu mingled with Nojima's feelings for Sugiko.

Other people might consider it nothing more than a stupid fantasy or deluded misconception.

Maybe I hadn't understood Miu's feelings.

But there was nothing false in my love for her.

Facing Sugiko at the Ping-Pong table, gripping the paddle tightly, we shot balls back and forth.

There was a smile of enjoyment on the face of the girl he loved. Each time she swung the paddle, the long sleeves of her kimono fluttered like butterflies' wings.

I was sure Nojima would have wished for this moment to go on forever.

"Where else would I find a woman so innocent, beautiful, and pure, so considerate, and so lovely? God is offering this woman to me. How cruel He would be otherwise."

"Where does this happiness come from? Is this illusion? It is much too rich for that."

"I cannot but love her; I cannot lose her. I will not be denied. God, have pity on me. Grant us our happiness."

But despite how much Nojima loved her, Sugiko loved his best friend Omiya.

Omiya had always been aware of the feelings Sugiko had for him. So he always treated her coolly. Ironically, that only attracted Sugiko to him even more.

"Why don't I stand in for Nojima?"

Omiya faced Sugiko across the Ping-Pong table. As he acted out Omiya pelting Sugiko with merciless shots, Akutagawa's expression was tense and forbidding. The conflict Omiya was feeling came through with almost painful clarity.

It was Akutagawa's own conflict and his own suffering, as well.

After the incident six years earlier, he had vowed to be always honorable and intelligent.

After he started high school, he must have felt so conflicted when Igarashi asked him to introduce him to Sarashina and when Sarashina told him she wanted to break up with Igarashi. He must have agonized over his decisions.

It must have tortured Akutagawa that he couldn't return Sarashina's feelings, though he felt how strong they were, and his guilt toward Igarashi must have wrenched his heart.

He had hidden those feelings for an entire year beneath a placid exterior, and never letting slip any complaint, he would only open up to his mother, who slumbered at the hospital, through the letters he wrote to her.

I didn't want to deny his awkwardness, his almost obstinate honor.

No matter how foolish it might be, no matter how mistaken.

You chose that path after careful consideration.

The story was approaching its climax.

Omiya was going abroad in order to sever his attachment to Sugiko.

"I pray for your happiness," he said with a quiet smile to Nojima, who had come to see him off.

Sugiko watched Omiya as he said that, tears springing to her eyes.

Our emotions mingling—

With Nojima's, with Omiya's, with Sugiko's—

Until I see myself in the people living inside the story as I read it.

Until I rejoice alongside them, laugh alongside them, feel sad, suffer, shout, and cry as I turn the pages.

Nojima proposes to Sugiko, but she turns him down.

Pressing the plaster mask of Beethoven that Omiya has sent

from overseas to my face, I crouched in the center of the stage and sobbed out Nojima's feelings.

Heartbreak is truly an awful thing.

I didn't know how I was supposed to overcome this unbearable pain that dashed my hopes in an instant, that covered the world in darkness, that cut my heart to shreds.

God—why did you take away the only thing that mattered to me?

Miu—I still haven't forgotten you. Every time I think of you, my breath catches, and I feel my chest tearing apart. Why did you refuse me and go so far away?!

Darkness fell over the stage, and Omiya stood at stage left, his face filled with anguish. A dim light illuminated him.

"Dear, honored friend. I owe you an apology. You will understand everything if you look at the story that appears in a certain literary magazine. I will not compel you to read it. It is my confession. And I ask you to judge us."

A spotlight fell over me as I huddled in the center of the stage. I looked down at a handmade magazine and flipped through the pages avidly.

Sugiko appeared at stage right and turned a tormented gaze toward Omiya, who stood at stage left.

Then lit by faint spotlights, Omiya and Sugiko began to alternately read the letters published in the magazine.

"Please don't be angry, Mister Omiya. It took all of my courage to write to you."

Tohko's clear voice spoke ardently of Sugiko's passion for Omiya.

In contrast, Omiya stubbornly refused her and begged her to accept his best friend Nojima.

"You are still unaware of the good in Nojima. I hope you will recognize his soul."

"Please, Mister Omiya, I want you to see me as an independent human being, as a woman. I want you to forget about Mister Nojima. I am the only one here."

"You are idealizing me. Even presuming that you came to be with me, it would not make you happy."

"You are a liar. Truly a liar."

The tense exchange continued.

Tohko's voice was colored by passion, her cheeks burning scarlet and her eyes filling with fiery tears as the lights shone on her.

In contrast, Akutagawa's expression slowly grew darker and firmer.

"I don't know how I should reply to you. I am at a loss. I wish I could talk to Nojima. But I lack the necessary courage. I feel so bad for him."

With each word he spoke, Akutagawa furrowed his brow in pain. His tightly balled fists were trembling.

Akutagawa's suffering pierced my heart.

The commandment he imposed on himself to be honorable, the terror of making a decision.

The events of the past had hog-tied him and pinned him down mercilessly.

Please don't give up. Cast off your commandment.

You're not a bad person.

You were honorable.

I want you to find a way to move on.

"I wondered whether to send this letter or if I had better not. I think it would be better not to. However —"

He stopped.

Akutagawa's face contorted, he opened his eyes wide and stared out at the audience as if he'd just suffered a terrible shock.

In the third row from the front, right in the middle, sat Mayuri Sarashina with bandages wrapped around her neck.

I gasped, too.

She was looking up at Akutagawa with agony in her face.

Akutagawa stiffened, his slightly open lips trembling. Then he squeezed his eyes shut and cradled his head in both hands, breathing in short gasps.

He looked exactly the way I did when I was having an attack.

The entire auditorium fell silent.

If he'd been unable to say his line so far, then there was no way Akutagawa could say it now, especially with Sarashina in front of him.

I wanted to run to him, but here onstage it was impossible. Just as I felt my chest constricting, a clear voice rang forth.

"Mister Omiya, will you let me tell you my story?"

Sugiko — no, Tohko had moved out to the center of the stage.
What are you doing, Tohko?!

The spotlight chased after her, appearing to be panicked at her unplanned movement.

"This story contains a very important 'truth' that will help you in your decision. Please hear me out, and don't plug your ears against me."

In the very center of the brilliant light, her long black hair swishing, her eyes glinting like stars, Tohko began to tell her tale.

"The main character is a boy who is polite and noble, an honor student skilled as both a scholar and an athlete.

"There are two other characters. Both are in the same school year as the boy. One is a serious girl with long hair, of a similar type to the boy. The other is a girl with short hair and cold eyes who we would have to call unfriendly.

"Both of them loved the boy."

Akutagawa raised his head and looked at Tohko in surprise.

Sarashina's eyes widened, too, and her face grew troubled.

Did the audience think this was part of the play? They stared transfixed at the stage, drawn in by Tohko's voice and movements, despite how dubious they looked.

On the other hand, I too was watching Tohko from onstage.

How would the book girl analyze Akutagawa's story, which was filled with hurt and lamentation?

Would Tohko be able to draw Omiya's line out of him?

"At the start of the second term, sparked by the fact that their seats were next to each other, the boy became friends with the long-haired girl. The long-haired girl didn't get along with her mother, and she was upset. The boy listened to her troubles and gave her his sister's old books and otherwise cheered her up.

"The short-haired girl watched the two of them bitterly, always from a slight distance. So the boy mistakenly thought that the short-haired girl hated him.

"But in fact, though the short-haired girl liked the boy more than she could bear, the long-haired girl and the boy seemed like the perfect honor student couple. She couldn't stand idly by."

The audience was hanging on her story, which seemed to have no connection whatsoever to the main plot.

The auditorium was as silent as a forest at night, Tohko's clear voice the only sound flowing into it.

"There was something the short-haired girl wanted. A rabbit doll. This rabbit was a love charm, and she had been told that if she had it, the boy she liked would return her feelings. The short-haired girl probably lingered outside the store festooned with these rabbits and begged her mother for one. And finally she got one.

"Maybe now the boy would notice her. The short-haired girl was ineffably happy. But the long-haired girl had the same rabbit doll.

"What's more, it had been a gift from the boy.

"The short-haired girl was so horribly aggrieved, so horribly sad, that she shoved the long-haired girl into a pond."

It was obvious that the main character was supposed to be Akutagawa, the long-haired girl was supposed to be Kanomata, and the short-haired girl was supposed to be Sarashina.

Partway through the story, Sarashina clasped her hands tightly together in her lap and bent her head in pain.

Tohko's story continued.

"But the long-haired girl, his best friend, is not the one the boy cares for; rather, he cares for the short-haired girl."

Sarashina's eyes shot up toward the stage.

I gaped, too.

The boy liked the short-haired girl? But that would mean that in elementary school, Akutagawa had liked Sarashina!

Akutagawa stared at Tohko, wide-eyed. I couldn't tell if his expression was one of confirmation or denial.

Tohko smiled.

"Do you not believe me, Mister Omiya? Do you laugh my story off as the fantasy of a book girl? I am not telling it absent of proof, you know.

"What you should pay attention to here is the rabbit doll.

"The boy confessed to another friend that it was a birthday gift. He was too shy to go by himself to a store frequented by girls, so he went to buy it with the long-haired girl and had her choose it.

"That by itself would make you think that he gave the rabbit doll to the long-haired girl for her birthday, no?

"But that makes no sense," Tohko declared, turning her majestic gaze on the audience. The audience had grown even quieter, and everyone was holding their breath, waiting for Tohko's next words.

Sarashina may as well have turned to stone.

"At this point, I'll give you a hint. The name of the long-haired girl was Emi, meaning 'smile.' Her father had given her this name because when she was born 'the mountains smiled.'

"Mister Omiya, if you have any knowledge of poetry, you should know what 'the mountains smiling' refers to. It is a seasonal allusion to spring when plants have begun to bud and the mountains appear lightly splashed with color. Which means that the long-haired girl was born in the spring. The long-haired girl grew close with the boy after summer vacation. He gave her the rabbit doll near the end of autumn. Long before her birthday.

"So then why did the boy tell his friend that it was a birthday gift?

"Did the boy lie?

"No. Can we not imagine that the rabbit was originally meant to be a birthday gift for someone else? The boy was embarrassed to go to the store alone, so he had the long-haired girl *come with him to select a gift for someone else.*

"And the short-haired girl's birthday was in the autumn, and moreover she had wanted that rabbit for a long time."

Astonishment showed on Sarashina's face as she stared at the stage.

And on Akutagawa's face, too.

Dressed in her fluttering sleeves and billowing pants, Tohko built her story up with a breezy rhythm.

The oppressive, torturous story was gradually tinged a lighter, gentler color.

"No, Mister Omiya? You always treated me coldly, but for that very reason, I became obsessed with you. Each time you were curt with me, I became sad and was even more captivated by you.

"Perhaps this boy was like me? Perhaps he was interested in the short-haired girl who only glared from afar and never came any closer?

"Then when by some chance the girl showed him some kindness or vulnerability, perhaps he fell in love with that aspect, which was so different from how she usually acted. That's how I picture it."

I recalled what Akutagawa had told me on a walk home one evening.

"If a girl shows me a side of herself that surprises me, I'm hooked. Like if I see a girl who's usually strong and willful crying when she's alone."

Maybe Akutagawa had seen Sarashina like that long ago. And maybe he had been captivated by it.

Akutagawa had been staring at Tohko in open shock, but now he lowered his eyes and looked desolate. Was he remembering Sarashina?

Tohko's tone also became pensive.

"The rabbit doll was a birthday gift for the short-haired girl. But perhaps since the short-haired girl already had one, the boy couldn't give it to her? Then the rabbit, which was no longer of any use, fell into the hands of the long-haired girl. Maybe the long-haired girl told him she would take it. Or maybe the long-haired girl knew all along that the short-haired girl already had the rabbit…

"The reason being that the short-haired girl was the long-haired girl's rival for the boy's love.

"So maybe she showed the rabbit she'd gotten to the short-haired girl and said that it was from the boy. This is nothing but conjecture, but…no matter how young she may be, a woman is still a woman. Some will do things like that."

With a sad expression, her eyes drooping, Tohko continued her story.

"The long-haired girl had to transfer to another school. But before she did, she went to see the short-haired girl and gave her the book and the rabbit she'd received from the boy, asking her to return them to him. Then she apologized.

"Why didn't the long-haired girl return them directly to the boy? Why did she deliberately entrust them to the short-haired girl? I feel that this also shows that the long-haired girl knew who the boy liked and that she felt sorry for taking the rabbit for herself."

Sarashina's face had grown melancholy as she watched Tohko.

Six years ago in elementary school, Sarashina had sliced off the rabbit's head, cut "Tangerines" out of the book, and sent them both to Akutagawa.

But it was inevitable. She had suffered and been terribly hurt herself.

Her long sleeves swooping, Tohko turned back to face Akutagawa.

"Well, Mister Omiya? You may be suspicious of how this story relates to you. But in the story of these children is hidden a very important truth that will allow you to carve out a new future for yourself here and now.

"Mister Omiya, you are afraid to accept me.

"Thus, you are afraid of a future that's different.

"From the very bottom of your soul, you are afraid that your decision will destroy everything, will cast it all into disarray!

"Although you are more honorable than anyone, you are essentially like that little boy, afraid that through your own foolishness you will make the wrong decision!

"But Mister Omiya! Who can decide whether the future of those wounded children now scattered to the winds will be harsh and gloomy? Who knows — maybe a brilliant future is opening up before them!"

Shock crossed Akutagawa's face.

Looking straight back at his shock, the book girl proclaimed loudly and powerfully, "When you close the book, does the story end? No! That's such a bland way to read. Every story goes on forever in our imaginations, and its characters live on.

"We can make those stories be full of shining light, or we can make them sad and desolate. That is why I, the book girl, imagine a wonderful future for those children!

"I'm positive that the long-haired girl is somewhere new and that she has recovered from her sadness, has reconciled with her parents, and is starting over feeling as if she's been reborn!

"The short-haired girl has been through another tragedy, has lost someone important to her, and has even hurt herself, but even so she'll have so many unbelievably happy experiences in her life simply because the future will make things right. I'm sure she'll enjoy every day of her life, that she'll struggle ahead, that lots of people will love her, and that she'll love them back with all her heart."

Like a ray of light breaking through a gap in the clouds, Tohko's strong, kind voice rang out regally.

"Well, Mister Omiya?

"We are all tied to many other things. To our families, our friends, our lovers; to anger, joy, sadness, hatred!

"All of those things are necessary to someone, and they might think that they would die if they cut them off. But people are born into this world by cutting the cord that ties them to their mother. There are futures you can never embark upon without severing your ties.

"There are things you can only learn by breaking everything apart or by hurting others. There are vistas that come into view the same way. And hearts.

"While the story I just told you tells of human foolishness and sadness, it is also a story of rebirth, a story of beginnings! A bright future is waiting with open arms. That's what that story is! And our story, also…"

A flush spread over Tohko's cheeks, and her eyes glinted like vibrant stars.

Her voice was filled with a bright hope.

Akutagawa listened to the future Tohko told him about with simple shock in his eyes. In the audience, Sarashina was trembling and weeping.

"Are you aware of the amazing Doctor Truth who appears in the story of a famous White Birch Society author? In his pursuit of truth and beauty, he says the following: 'If you never throw your hands up in defeat in your life, you will never know what's true! When there are things you can't bear, it's all right to just cry! Things we can bear have no power to reform us. It's because there are things in life we can't bear that humans can be reborn!'

"Through his many stories, the author who sent Doctor Truth out into the world sang the praises of the strength and goodness people have. He believed in people, loved people, and wrote stories of rebirth in straightforward, unaffected language!

"Of course, there are times when you're unable to believe in yourself, let alone other people, and there will be setbacks and failures. Everyone carries with them their own pain and confusion and suffering. No one is free from troubles. No one is free from suffering. No one in the world is free from failing at least once!

"Because human beings are all fools!

"Me and you and the characters in every creative work ever made and the flesh-and-blood people living in the world—all of them have something about them that's foolish.

"If people weren't fools, they could never create art or literature! All of us, every single one, is a fool!

"Schools and society are just groups of fools. You need to understand that first of all!"

The dark shadows in Akutagawa's eyes faded, as if he was slowly waking up from a nightmare at the dawn after a long, long night.

His tensed jaw relaxed, and a refreshed expression came over his face that seemed to wash away all his pain and suffering.

Tohko had used all her strength to tell him that.

In the darkness, she was strikingly illuminated by the spotlight.

Her glossy black hair, her sweat-soaked cheek and forehead, the line of her neck—all glistened like they were inlaid with stars from the night sky. Without pausing for an instant, still strong, her pink lips continued to weave together words of warmth.

"Don't worry about everything that could possibly happen and then freeze up because you're trying to be clever! Don't be prisoner to the chains that bind you!

"Try imagining something happy, that the future is bright and wonderful! Your imagination might go too far and you might

fail, or you might feel pathetic or embarrassed, and of course it's wrong to hurt people for a mistaken dream. But if you make a mistake and stumble, you should get back up and keep walking!

"Even if painful things happen, the future will only make it right for you in the end, so don't get discouraged. We're all fools anyway, so be a fool who holds ideals in your heart. Be a fool who acts without being afraid of failure.

"It's all right to be a fool. Speak your mind, your truth, to your heart's content and in your own way with your voice and your words! Decide in your heart on the path you'll take!"

A warmly lit sky at sunset filled my mind.

A bright, soft, orange-colored sky...

First one, then another vividly colored tangerine tossed up at it.

Tohko's pale hands throwing tangerines one after another into the evening sky, arcing overhead.

Three. Four. Five.

With a sunny smile, with kind eyes, with her braids swinging, laughing in a bright voice —

The gloom lodged in my heart melted away in a tangy fragrance.

Akutagawa's jaw was set, and there was a flash of decisiveness in his eyes.

"I will send him a letter. Forgive me, Nojima."

He had whispered the words quietly but distinctly.

It was Akutagawa's break from the past.

I heard it and so did Sarashina.

Sarashina was no longer trembling. Her cheeks were streaked with tears, but she lifted her face and watched the stage with something like a prayer in her eyes.

Straightening his back, Akutagawa threw a hand out toward Tohko and shouted, his face burning with passion, "My beloved angel, come to Paris with Takeko. Send me every picture of you since you were a baby. Even if it costs me the world, I would not lose you. But if I gain all the world with you by my side, what fortune — what fortune that would be."

A smile split Tohko's face, spreading exquisitely over her features.

Her long black hair spread like wings as she ran to Akutagawa. The spotlight chased after her.

Then the light shining on Akutagawa and the light shining on Tohko mingled and pooled into one spotlight. Tohko spread her arms wide, her face erupting with joy, and threw herself against Akutagawa's chest with the force of a tackle and hugged him.

"Thank you! Thank you, Mister Omiya! Thank you!"

Normally the scene should have had Sugiko slowly walking toward Omiya with a smile and Omiya approaching Sugiko; then Sugiko would gently rest her hand in Omiya's, and the two would look into each other's eyes and smile.

But Tohko was probably much too happy.

Akutagawa's eyes bugged out when she embraced him unexpectedly, but his face quickly brightened, and he gently hugged her back.

As far as the story went, it had been a flawless performance of an iconic scene. But to be honest, watching it flaunted right in front of me made me jealous.

You're too excitable, Tohko.

Maybe the reason my heart throbbed and I started to feel bitter and forlorn was that I had synced up with Nojima's emotions.

Darkness fell over the stage, and the joyous lovers disappeared into shadow.

A light overhead picked me out, crouched in the center of the empty stage and gaping down at the magazine I held open.

Omiya had gained the woman he loved best in exchange for

friendship, but Nojima had lost his best friend and the woman he loved in one blow. It was difficult to confront that pain, that despair, that suffering.

But as Tohko had said, there are futures you can't embark upon without severing your ties.

There are things you can only discover by breaking everything apart or by hurting others. There are vistas that come into view the same way. And hearts.

Now I, too, wanted to believe that.

That beyond the darkness, a new world was opening up.

That even if we passed each other by, even if we insulted each other, even if we beat each other apart, even if we were separated, even if we hurt and were hurt, we would be able to join hands again some day — I wanted to believe that relationships like that existed.

So I wouldn't be afraid to make decisions anymore, either.

I tore the magazine in half and stood up, then threw the mask Omiya had sent against the stage.

The plaster mask shattered loudly and sent white chips flying.

I screamed at the audience, as if breaking the heavy chains that had bound me until now. "I can endure this alone. And something will be born of this loneliness. Perhaps a time will come when I will shake your hands on a mountaintop. But until then, the two of us will walk different paths."

The strength went out of my legs, and I collapsed once more to the stage.

In the light that gradually faded and disappeared, I bowed my head and held it, moaning in a low voice.

"I have at last withstood loneliness. Must I endure even more now, utterly alone? Help me, Lord."

I would probably burrow into my bed and cry again.

I would probably have regrets and disappointments.

I can't face this pain — I would probably think that, too.

But even so, a person cries, and then afterward they get back up and start walking again.

That's when their real story begins.

As I huddled in the darkness, the sound of copious applause and cheers reached my ears, rocking the auditorium.

Epilogue – Friends

After the play was over, Sarashina came to the classroom that served as our dressing room. Her eyes were bright red and blood-shot, but something in her face was liberated and refreshed.

"I'm sorry for causing all that trouble. I'll stay away from you, Akutagawa...I was afraid of being alone. All my parents do is fight, and ever since I was little I've spent my birthdays by myself. I wanted someone to celebrate my birthday with me. But after I saw your play, I felt like I would be fine on my own now."

"I'm the one who should apologize."

Akutagawa bowed to Sarashina.

Sarashina and Akutagawa...they both seemed a little lonely.

"Hey, there's something I want you two to see," Tohko said brightly, holding out an essay collection from some middle school. "I actually wanted Akutagawa to read this before the play started, but then Nanase fainted and we were running all over the place, and I missed my chance. Read the page with the bookmark."

Akutagawa accepted the book dubiously, then opened it to the page with the violet-colored bookmark.

The rest of us peeked in from the sides.

When we did, we glimpsed the handwritten name and title on the page.

"Picking Tangerines"   Emi Kanomata   Class 1, Year 2

"Is this an essay by Kanomata?"

Tohko smiled.

Akutagawa and Sarashina began to read it voraciously.

"On Sunday, my mother and father and I went to pick tangerines at the orchard nearby."

The essay began with that one sentence, spinning a tender scene of a family enjoying themselves picking tangerines. It went on to say this:

We were all eating tangerines together, and I remembered a story by Ryunosuke Akutagawa called "Tangerines." I read the story a long time ago with a friend of mine, and right after I changed schools, I would read it over and over whenever I felt lonely and it cheered me up. It was a very important story to me, and it is my favorite.

As Akutagawa and Sarashina read the essay, smiles touched with melancholy came over their faces.

Tohko murmured gently, "The future I talked about onstage had a little bit of truth mixed in."

Kanomata had been unable to vent her depression about her parents except by cutting up textbooks, but living somewhere new, she had reconciled with them and was living at peace.

Kanomata was no longer unhappy and didn't hold a grudge

against anyone. She cherished the days gone by as warm memories.

I was sure that finding that out meant that Akutagawa and Sarashina could both be happy and at ease.

Like seeing tangerines bobbing against a sunset…

That was how their faces looked.

"I hated Ryunosuke Akutagawa's 'Tangerines,'" Sarashina murmured. "But I'll try reading it again. I bet I'll feel differently when I read it now."

Sarashina started to leave, but Akutagawa called her back.

"Konishi—I had Kanomata choose that rabbit to give you for your birthday. That part was true, too. I went past your house once, and I saw you crying alone in your yard, and after that I started to like you."

Akutagawa had called her Konishi—not Sarashina.

At the hospital, I'd asked Akutagawa if he liked Sarashina, and he had gotten a melancholy look on his face and responded, "I used to."

I guess that had been the unvarnished truth. It wasn't just a sense of guilt, but the fact that he had liked her when they were little that made it impossible for Akutagawa to cut Sarashina off.

Sarashina's eyes teared up ever so slightly, and she smiled.

"Thank you. Good-bye, Kazushi."

Immediately after Sarashina left, Maki came in to replace her.

"Well done! You were great onstage, Tohko! I enjoyed every minute of it, so I'll forgive you for making *me* waitress at your curry restaurant dressed as a maid."

"You actually did it?! Dressed as a maid?" I shouted, aghast.

"Have I ever refused one of Tohko's requests?" Maki replied brazenly. "Oh yes, Tohko! That profligate boy whose family you're living with? He stopped by the restaurant."

"You mean Ryuto?"

"Yes. With a herd of girls around him. That kid hasn't changed. When I went to take his order, he actually recoiled and his eyes bugged out, and he said, 'Now there's a hair-raisin' sight,' so I kicked the leg of his chair and knocked him over."

She smiled captivatingly.

When I imagined this girl dressed as a maid and welcoming customers to her restaurant, I felt hugely sympathetic to Ryuto's outburst. Though if I said so, she might kick me, too.

"Thank you, Maki. For the play and everything else, too. I'm really glad you were there."

Tohko usually avoided Maki as much as possible, but she thanked her with odd humility and bowed her head.

Maki must have used her connections to get the essay collection and had given it to Tohko.

But what had the "compensation" been?

Maki's eyes glinted with satisfaction.

"Has my love finally gotten through to you? If I asked you right now, would you get naked for me?"

"I would not!" Tohko shouted, her face bright red, and Maki grinned.

"Oh well. Too bad. I've gotten enough in 'compensation,' anyway."

Tohko sputtered.

Maki drew her face closer to mine and whispered, "The orchestra is giving a concert in the main hall soon. You should definitely come, Konoha. You'll see something fun."

"Heeey, what are you telling him?!"

Tohko thrashed her long kimono sleeves around in a frenzy. Maki gave her an affectionate wink and left the room.

"Huh? Something fun? I wonder what that means?"

Takeda cocked her head behind me. She'd overheard Maki.

"N-never mind, Chia. Forget about it! And you, Konoha, are absolutely forbidden to go to the concert!"

*　　*　　*

There was a huge rush to change back into our uniforms after that; then Takeda and Akutagawa said they needed to get back to their classes, and we parted ways. I ran to the music hall where the concert would be.

Tohko chased right behind me in her uniform and uneven braids.

"Are you really going? Why? Classical music will just put you to sleep. Wouldn't you rather go get anmitsu fruit salad with me?"

"You can't eat that, though."

"Then we could just go back to the club room, and you could write a love story that tastes like it for your beloved president."

"I don't want to bother with your treats in the middle of the fair."

"Why do you want to go to the orchestra's concert so badly?"

"A better question is why you're following me when you're so out of breath."

"But, but, but —"

Tohko balled her hands into fists as she ran and flailed her head and elbows back and forth in babyish refusal. Despite this tug-of-war, we reached the hall in the middle of campus.

"Nooo! Don't go innnn!"

Tohko grabbed the cuff of my uniform sleeve and tried desperately to hold me back, but I bought tickets and went in with her still hanging on.

In the lobby, there was a billboard so big I had to look up to see it all.

It was a blown-up photo of Tohko.

Dressed like a cheerleader in a tank top and miniskirt, she held two pom-poms in her hands and was leaping in the air with a smile on her face. Her hair was in ponytails and — whether it was something Maki was into or something Tohko had wanted — she wore a big pair of glasses.

Her chest, covered by the sheer tank top, was spectacularly flat, and her white skin peeked out from under the bottom of it. It was a risky angle that almost, but not quite showed her belly button, and then in addition to that, her pleated skirt stopped right at the point where it very nearly almost, but not quite showed her underwear. Her white legs were bent, knees together, as she hung in the air.

Beside the billboard stood a slogan that read, "THE SEIJOH ACADEMY ORCHESTRA PRESENTS: A RALLYING CRY TO THE FUTURE."

So this was the "compensation" this time around.

Actually, I was pretty sure I'd spotted Tohko running somewhere in a big hurry with her hair in strangely uneven braids before. Had that been after the photo shoot?

I was looking up at the billboard, convinced, while beside me Tohko turned bright red from the back of her neck to the tips of her ears and wailed, "N-no, Konoha...that's not me. It's someone from another class. Please, don't look...Don't look, Konoha."

I chuckled. "You must be happy, then. There's someone else just as flat chested as you."

I felt an immediate bomp on my head.

"How mean! What a heartless kid! And after I lent you that handkerchief!"

"That was my handkerchief. Look, the concert's starting. Besides, people are staring."

I noticed the people in the lobby whispering, "Hey, it's the girl in the picture," and Tohko buried her face against my back.

"L-let's hurry, and go get a seat, Konoha."

This is just making them stare even more...

She kept her face buried, clutching fistfuls of my shirt in both hands, and I started walking off in resignation. Her warmth against my back felt ever so slightly ticklish.

"Grrrr. I am never, *ever* agreeing to do something for Maki *ever* again!"

Tohko continued growling even after we'd taken our seats.

"That reminds me, how's your bear hunter boyfriend doing?" I asked, suddenly remembering. Her eyes went wide, her face turned bright red, and she reeled back.

"Wh-wh-wh-wh-wh-wh-whadddya mean?"

"Winter starts early in Hokkaido, so he'll need his white scarf soon."

"Urk—"

"Send me an invitation when you have your ceremony in the chapel. With a round-trip ticket attached."

Tohko faltered, her cheeks still coloring; then she glowered at me, her eyes vulnerable.

"K-Konoha! You are despicable!"

Finally the curtain lifted, and the orchestra that was the pride of Seijoh Academy began its concert.

Maki was actually giddy and seemed to be enjoying herself, dressed in tails and waving her baton.

When the orchestra's inspiring concert was over and we'd gone back outside, the campus was dyed in a gentle sunset.

"The closing ceremonies are beginning. All students please assemble in the gymnasium."

The announcement from the event coordinators flowed through the orange-colored sky.

Tohko and I split up, and I went back to my classroom, where Akutagawa was standing by himself at a window, gazing at the view outside.

"Akutagawa?"

"Inoue…"

215

Akutagawa turned to look at me, and I walked over to stand beside him.

"You're not going to the closing ceremonies?"

"It makes me strangely sad that the culture fair is ending. I was off in a reverie."

"I never thought I'd hear you say something like that."

A chilly wind blew in through the open window.

The classroom was painted the same color as the setting sun.

"But maybe I'm the same way. It's like there's a crack in my heart now. It's not necessarily a bad sensation... I was in suspense all day long, but it was still fun," I said.

Akutagawa smiled. "It was."

This congenial mood was pleasant; I wanted to immerse myself in it forever.

"You know, after I started high school, I was never really into school events like this. I thought they were a pain, and I just needed to get through them. But... I'm glad I went onstage with you."

"I was like you, too, Inoue. For me, the culture fair, the sports day, student life in general — they were nothing more than a duty that had to be carried out. I never did anything with friends and enjoyed myself like this. It's thanks to you and Amano that I could experience that feeling."

"Tohko was the one who got the lines out of you. I didn't do anything."

"No, if you hadn't told me that we would face it together, I would have run away before I ever went onstage."

"Really? Because you definitely didn't run away. But if I managed to help you out, I'm glad."

Akutagawa smiled, his face refreshed. It was a smile that only someone who has overcome their pain could make. He had broken his chains with his own hands and had started moving toward the future.

And I had, too.

"I'd like to be your friend, Akutagawa."

Akutagawa's eyes widened just a little, and a look of surprise came over his face.

"I've been avoiding getting close to people. Something hurt me awhile ago, and I didn't want to get hurt by being close to anyone ever again. You and I have a lot in common. But now, I'd like to be closer with you. Could you be my friend, Akutagawa?"

His bulging eyes dropped slightly, and he looked troubled.

"There are still some things I can't talk about, Inoue. I might hurt you eventually."

His confession surprised me.

What secrets could Akutagawa have locked away in his heart? About his mother? Or maybe —

Questions bubbled up one after another, but I gave him a smile.

"I don't mind. If you don't want to talk about it, you can keep it a secret forever."

Akutagawa raised his face.

Once more, surprise spread over his handsome, masculine features.

I held out my hand.

"Let's be friends. Even if we fight or part ways eventually, for now I want to be your friend."

Akutagawa watched me, his eyes still wide.

I submitted myself to his gaze.

Even if he hurt me or if I hurt him, something new would come out of it — a bond that would mature.

Believe that —

Akutagawa's eyes crinkled warmly.

Then he reached out a big hand and powerfully gripped mine.
His hand was flushed with heat. I squeezed it back firmly.
There was no need to acknowledge this with words.
We were friends now.

———◇———

It's been a long time since I wrote to you.

In these last two months, I've received many letters from you, but I haven't been able to respond. I hope you can forgive me.

In your letters, you write repeatedly for me to come see you and I can tell that you're annoyed at me, but there were circumstances that kept me from visiting you.

To be honest, I was afraid to face you.

I met you last winter. In the third term of my first year.

I'd come to visit my mom and got to know you because you were staying at the same hospital.

You were all alone in the hall, practicing walking.

You stumbled and fell many times, but you would get back up and start walking unsteadily; then you would fall again, then start walking again. Your body wouldn't do what you wanted it to, and you were getting awfully frustrated with it. You muttered bitterly to yourself a lot, and it looked like you were crying a little.

That glimpse of your tears stuck in my mind, and after that I would hide around the corner almost every day and watch you walking, utterly incapable of speaking to you.

Then one day after you'd fallen down in the hallway just like you always did, still crumpled up on all fours on the floor, you said something in bitter irritation.

"You're always standing there peeping out at me. I'm not a freak show."

Can you imagine how shocked I was?

How I felt like a sly blade had stabbed me in the chest when you then lifted your face and glared at me, and I saw violent rage and hatred burning in your eyes? How you took me prisoner in that moment?

As I apologized, you assaulted me with cold remarks and tried to put me at a distance.

Even after that, whenever I would go to see you and try to talk to you, you looked unhappy and tried to distance yourself from me.

If I tried to help you, your rage would flare, and you insisted that you could do everything on your own, that you didn't want pity from someone like me, that you didn't want me to help you out.

I told you how I felt, knowing that you would be angry.

I had from the beginning overlaid your image with the girl I'd hurt long ago.

That girl was in the same grade as me in elementary school, and her name was Mayuri Konishi. I probably told you this story at some point.

Every time you insulted me, I felt as if she was attacking me. And so I was being redeemed a little by it.

That was because I believed I was someone who deserved to be attacked.

It gets a little complicated, but at the time I was going out with Konishi, whom I'd run into again in high school.

But she wasn't the way she used to be, and the way she had become made it utterly impossible for me to like her as simply a member of the opposite sex. And then the fact that it was a betrayal of my mentor, who was in love with her, might have also put a damper on my feelings for her.

Konishi looked at me with needy eyes that said it was enough for us just to be together, and she never complained or reproached me for feeling nothing for her. She relied on me and trusted me.

It was cowardly of me, but I felt she was a burden. Then I tasted an even more powerful guilt because of that.

So whenever loathing for me came over your face, which reminded me of the Konishi from my past, I felt that by accepting your punishment I was being forgiven and it calmed me, even as my heart snapped apart and I felt such pain I thought it would choke me.

And so I was even more drawn to you.

At first you simply despised me as you would a worm, but once you found out that I was a first-year at Seijoh Academy, you became eager for my visits. Then you started asking me all sorts of things about school. It was to get information out of me about a person who lived on in your heart with a biting pain.

You told me, your eyes burning with hatred, that he had hurt you deeply and stolen your future from you.

After I started my second year and moved into the same class as him, you and I became closer than ever. At the same time, our relationship transformed into something much more difficult for me to bear.

Even worse, you ran into him at the hospital.

When I came to your room a few days before summer break, you were pale and you told me how he had come to the hospital.

Apparently he'd come to visit a classmate. You asked me obsessively who the girl with him had been, and whether he was close to the person he was visiting since she was a girl, too, and what their relationship was to each other.

After that day, you started acting strangely.

When I thought you were staring absently out a window, your temper would flare suddenly or you'd get horribly annoyed or start crying or screaming or hitting me.

One day when I went to see you, you were lying in bed ripping sheets of paper into tiny pieces.

You had told me you wanted to write letters and asked me to buy that paper for you.

Maybe you were planning to send him a letter on your favorite stationery.

I guess you had some sort of internal conflict, and you'd torn up the letter you'd started writing.

As you ripped the letter up, your eyes flashed with uncontrollable irritation and hatred, and there was blood on your lip. Probably because you'd bitten down on it so hard. There were traces of tears on your cheeks.

Then predictably, you pressured me to help you get revenge on him.

You probably realized yourself that it was closer to a threat than a request.

You were prepared to use any means necessary to draw me in as an ally, and you screamed that if I wouldn't hear you out, you would cut your wrists and die; you tried indecent acts on me, called me a coward for not doing what you told me to, and threw things.

Then when I stopped going to the hospital, you started sending me letters almost every day.

Since I knew only too well how much determination and strenuous effort it cost you to write so much, it haunted me even more to see the stationery turned black with so many typed-out words and the haltingly handwritten address on the envelope.

I should have set the letters aside unopened, but to my despair, I had already started to have feelings for you, not as a replacement for Konishi, but for yourself.

You might actually commit an act that would end your life.

It wrenched my heart to think that, and since I knew that you were capable of actually doing it, my suffering only deepened.

And then I thought, what if you were wallowing in sorrow, what if you were crying all alone, what if you were begging for my help? And I couldn't help but open the letters.

At some point I even started to believe that granting your wish might be atonement for the mistakes I'd committed in the past.

Not thinking anything for myself, listening only to your will, living only for you. If I could do that, how easy everything would be.

In fact, I did try to put a letter from you into his shoe locker once. I thought maybe if I did that, it would help me commit.

But there existed inside me, as unshakable as a boulder, a rationality that told me it was wrong to do that, and in the end I tore up the letter and threw it away.

Being an honorable person.

I think I told you how after that incident in the past, I've lived my life with that resolution in mind: that I had to be an honorable person at all times, and that I could never hurt anyone ever again.

And yet you asked that of me.

To betray a classmate and hurt him.

I can't listen to requests like that. It isn't honorable. But even as the annoyance and intensity of your letters increased,

Konishi was slowly going crazy from the inadequacy of my responses, and I was being driven into a corner.

I was frantic to save her somehow, but I was just spinning my wheels. Konishi's actions violated all reason, and she was approaching unassailable madness.

I barely managed to rein myself in by addressing the letters I would have sent you to my mother instead.

And that took me to my absolute limit. I was unable to save Konishi as she descended into madness, but even in a situation like that, I couldn't help thinking about you, which made me feel like an awful person. I felt such despair that it blacked out everything else in my mind.

I believed I was unworthy of seeing you as I was then. Even when I went to visit my mom, I couldn't stop by your room.

I've been suffering these last two months. I swear I haven't abandoned you. It's selfish of me to ask, but I want you to understand that at least, if nothing else. These last two months have been essential, at least for me.

Now that the issues with Konishi are resolved and I'm free from the past, I'm finally able to send you a letter.

I'll start with the conclusion.

I won't be able to drive him into a trap or demean him.

Because I've become friends with him. You are important to me, and so is he.

I may hurt him eventually because of you. But I want to be as honorable toward my friend as possible from now on. I don't want to set up traps or make any other cowardly acts against him.

I'm making that clear to you.

I've been unable to say something as simple as that to you these last two months, and I was caught in a loop of foolish acts like slicing your letters apart with a box cutter and cutting myself. I kept sending my replies to my mother.

I'm probably still a fool.

But someone taught me something: All people are fools.

So at least be a fool who acts with ideals in your heart.

And so I recognize the fool that I am, and with that knowledge I'd like to move toward you and toward him.

A week had gone by since the culture fair.

Our play had gotten good reviews, and messages of support trickled into the goblin mailbox—I mean, the love advice mailbox—in the school yard, saying things like "That was *really* good. I felt my heart just *ache*" and "Now I want to read Saneatsu Mushanokōji's books," which made Tohko happy.

She ripped up the notes she got from the mailbox and would bring them to her lips, beaming cheerily.

"Yummmm! It tastes exactly like sweet, freshly picked peaches—or maybe grapes—that you had to work hard to gather. I can feel it filling my belly with freshness!"

On the other hand, there were some notes mixed in that said things like "Let's see you dress up like a nurse" or "Next time, please slash Nojima and Omiya." She dutifully ate these, too, whining as she went.

"Urk, this is so weirrrrd. It's like roasted chestnuts and mashed sweet potatoes with *mayonnaise* on top! It's like smoked squid with condensed milk sprinkled *all over it*!"

"How has Akutagawa been?" Tohko asked me when I reached the club room after school, her legs pulled up on a fold-up chair as she read Chekhov's *The Cherry Orchard.*

"He's staying upbeat. He said that Igarashi came to the archery hall yesterday and apologized. Oh, there's a match next week, and I promised I'd go cheer them on. And then we found out we both like movies, so we're going to see one together sometime."

I told her various tidbits as I set my pen case and paper on the table.

"That's nice."

Her eyes softened, and the corners of her mouth curved into a smile like a violet blooming.

I felt a tickle deep in my chest.

Just then, Kotobuki popped in.

"Ummm...sorry to bother you. I just...wanted to apologize for what happened at the culture fair. So, uh, I made some more cookies. I want you to have them as my way of saying sorry."

She bowed to Tohko, then stole a glance at me and flushed.

"Oooooh, thank you, Nanase. I'll share these with Konoha, then. Why don't you join us?"

"*What*—?! Uh, no, I have library duty. I've gotta go."

"Oh. That's too bad."

"Next time, then, Kotobuki."

I smiled at her. Her eyes went wide, and she turned even redder.

"S-see you."

Then she speedily left the room. I thought she was kind of cute when she acted like that.

Hugging the bundle of neatly wrapped cookies to her chest, Tohko bent forward to peer up into my face and, a teasing glint in her eyes, she asked, "All right, Konoha, did something happen between you and Nanase?"

"I'm not telling."

"Ohhh, so something *did* happen!" she shouted and puffed her cheeks out indignantly.

I probably ought to sit down and talk to Kotobuki soon. Ask her where we met back in middle school.

"Come on, Konoha. You can tell your president. Just whisper it."

"I can't respond to private questions."

"Oh, I'm scandalized!"

"What's that supposed to mean? What are you picturing?"

Tohko whined, "No fair keeping secrets." But then she looked down at the bundle of cookies and sadly murmured, "I'm...lying to Nanase and to all the others, aren't I?"

Her sudden admission lodged into my heart.

Tohko untied the ribbon and opened the bundle. Cookies shaped like hearts and stars sat cheerfully atop a flower-print napkin, sending the fragrance of sugar and butter into the cramped room.

Sweet treats that Tohko couldn't taste.

She plucked out a star-shaped cookie with her slender fingers and tossed it into her mouth, chewed it hungrily, and then smiled brightly.

"I bet this tastes like Travers's *Mary Poppins*! Sweet, crunchy, and redolent of its almond topping!" she exclaimed breezily, then ate up one cookie after another, rhythmically chewing it up and swallowing it with a smile.

"This one tastes like Webster's *Daddy-Long-Legs*! The scent of lemon spreads so brightly over my tongue! This one tastes like Burnett's *The Secret Garden*! Like rose-colored jam that's sweet, tart, and totally romantic. Could this cookie with the tea leaves in it be *Alice in Wonderland*? The slightly bitter parts are the tastiest thing ever!"

Tohko was boundlessly cheerful and optimistic as she related what she imagined each cookie tasted like.

They were all impenetrable mysteries to her.

Secreting gloomy thoughts such as *I'm different from other people* away in her heart, Tohko pictured the flavors of sweet treats and beamed joyfully.

I was sure of the book girl's existence, and just like you and I, she laughs, and whines, and cries, and fails when she tries to do handstands, and leaps in the air dressed like a cheerleader, and cheers people up, and falls down, and gets back up.

I sat in a fold-up chair and flipped through the paper in the notebook I'd set on the table.

Then I started to write a treat whose sweetness Tohko would be able to appreciate.

My prompts today were "friends," "buddies," and "friendship"…

⟫◆⟪

Ms. Miu Asakura,

When this letter reaches you, I'll visit.
And I'll tell you the feelings I couldn't write in a letter, and tell you clearly and with my own voice about becoming friends with Konoha Inoue, who even now dominates your heart.

Kazushi Akutagawa

Afterword

Hello, Mizuki Nomura here. This is the third installment of the *Book Girl* series. We're right at the halfway point in the story, and even Konoha, who bursts into tears every time, has grown up a little bit.

The inspiration was Saneatsu Mushanokōji's *Friendship*. The protagonists of Mushanokōji's story are so passionate! They're a treasure house of famous lines! I can't say enough good things about his book! I drew from the source more than I usually have in this story, but there are spots where I tweaked things slightly for the play, so please don't be mad. I stayed true to the phrasing of the original as best I could. There are lots of famous lines I didn't have the space to introduce, though, so you should definitely get your hands on a copy of *Friendship* or any of his other stories and read it for yourself. I'm certain you'll encounter words that will echo through your soul.

This time, as usual, I felt terrible for poor little Kotobuki. She never has a very big role, and she keeps getting sidelined without ever getting involved in the central story. In a sense, she might be the most unfortunate person in the entire series. I'd like to try and do something for her in the next volume.

And now, the thank-yous.

Thank you to the illustrator, Miho Takeoka, for her always amazing drawings. The prefatory color drawings in the second installment were fantastic! In fact, in the yearly rankings of *This Light Novel Is Amazing!* which is published by Takarajimasha, the first installment of this series (*The Suicidal Mime*) was ranked first in the cover art category! Thanks to that, we managed to rank in the top ten for the overall category and character category, too. My editor was extremely pleased, and I was very happy, too. Thank you so much to everyone who voted for us.

I struggle over this series every time and I'm writing down to the very last second, but I've received a lot of encouragement and joy from it. I'm going to stay fired up and fighting till the very last volume, so I hope you'll stick around. Until next time.

Mizuki Nomura

December 3, 2006

AFTERWORD

While producing the pictures for volume 3, all this stuff happened and it was a desperate couple of days, but Ms. Nomura's powerful writing kept me moving, and now we've made it. Konoha did a good job . . . this time.

To the editor,
To the designer,
To everyone at the printer's, thanks a bunch.

I—I'll see you next time!!

Miho Takeoka

Yay, volume 3. It's yellow. I didn't mean for that to happen, but it just turned into a turn-of-the-century romance color all on its own.

This sketch was a candidate for an illustration in this book. I asked if I should put it in the afterword and got the absolute thumbs-up, so I'll stick it in.